POLITIQUETTE

POLITIQUETTE

The People's Guide to Political
Discourse in the New Millennium

Nadia Asencio

authorHOUSE®

AuthorHouse™
1663 Liberty Drive
Bloomington, IN 47403
www.authorhouse.com
Phone: 1 (800) 839-8640

Published by AuthorHouse 01/07/2016

ISBN: 978-1-5049-5721-2 (sc)
ISBN: 978-1-5049-5722-9 (e)

Library of Congress Control Number: 2015917422

Print information available on the last page.

Any people depicted in stock imagery provided by Thinkstock are models, and such images are being used for illustrative purposes only. Certain stock imagery © Thinkstock.

This book is printed on acid-free paper.

To my mother, with love and gratitude

Table of Contents

Prologue

"Friction retards progress." ~ James Cash Penney

Writing a book is a scary thing. First, there's the isolation; it takes time to write, time away from friends, family, and a thousand other opportunities that you could be spending your time pursuing, but which you must forgo if you're going to get the job done. Will you be able to pick up where you left off when your book is finished, or will you have missed out on something important and irretrievable? Then there's the fact that you're exposing your ideas to the world, putting them out there for anyone and everyone to criticize and attack. Sometimes, you'll offend those closest to you; inevitably, you'll offend people whom you've never met but who could still affect your life moving forward somehow. The fallout can be brutal. And of course, there's the biggest fear of all – that your work won't serve, that it will fall on deaf ears, that it will "Van Gogh." After all, if you've dedicated months of your life to writing it's because you felt a passionate need to share your story. It's what drives you to keep writing when nothing else can, when you've lost la joie de l'écriture and realize that the banality of writing 40,000-plus words takes a level of tenacity you aren't 100%

sure you can muster. But somehow, you do. Because the hope is that, when it's all over, your work *will* serve; that although it may offend some, it will benefit many more. That it will give voice to often-overlooked perspectives, that it will fulfill an urgent purpose. That although you did miss out on spending quality time with the people you love, you'll be able to replace that lost time with something valuable and timeless. That it won't all be for naught.

Understand, I grew up in a home of Cuban immigrants where politics was discussed *every* day; where happy social gatherings took place every week, and which always ended up hours later in boisterous political debates fueled by more than a few bottles of rum and a dozen hard-core ex-pats holding court in our large, Italian-tiled kitchen. The kids would hide on the second-floor stairwell, listening in on the adults as they went at it, often amazed at how passionate they got and also, surprised that none of the neighbors had called the police yet. Thanks to my Cuban heritage, politics has been a vital part of my life for as far back as I can remember.

My parents were members of "El Centro Civico Cubano," a social club that had been established by Cuban exiles when they migrated to Connecticut in the 70s and 80s (usually via Miami) in search of high paying jobs and the opportunity to start their lives anew; by consolidating their resources, they were able to achieve just that. Back then, Connecticut swelled with highly productive factories and Hartford was known as the "Insurance Capital of the World" – there were plenty of good-paying jobs for either blue- or white-collar workers, and there was a stellar public education system in place to instruct their children (Connecticut consistently ranks in the nation's top three states for education). Through hard work and the cooperation of their extended network in the "Cuban Club," my parents and their friends prospered and were able to afford to give us kids the opportunities that they had been robbed of in their own country.

Our parents' examples taught us that to get ahead you had to plan, sacrifice, and exert yourself to earn a better life, but also, that no one got ahead without the help of others; and that once we made any type of leeway in this world, it was then our obligation to extend a hand backward to help the next guy up. When I was younger I assumed everyone followed this creed, but the older I got I realize how rare it is to be raised this way, and how lucky I was to have had such a large, extended community teach me this valuable lesson growing up.

I wrote this book for the People, because I love my country and because I love my countrymen. I believe in the founding principles of this great nation, and I believe that if it's going to stand a chance of surviving this century intact, it's going to take a paradigm shift in the way that "We the People" relate to one another and to the powers that be. It should be apparent to all of us by now that there are many forces in our world today that are actively challenging our ability to adapt and move forward while simultaneously holding onto those principles that are most basic to our way of life; however, I don't think it's an impossible feat to accomplish. But it *is* going to take cooperation, and the ability to understand and accept our current realities.

We can't afford the fear that keeps us arguing amongst ourselves while others benefit at our expense; neither can we continue to buy into myths or toe the line for others. We must be willing to abandon the false security of rhetoric and ideology – those pacifiers that help us deal with the unknown, or worse, to turn a blind eye to the truth – and find the courage to examine the facts instead. Even more importantly, we have to be willing to accept that there even *is* an unknown in order to move beyond it, collecting pertinent intel (different perspectives, new information, and data) that will help us clarify what we're really dealing with. The minute we convince ourselves that we already have all the answers and cut ourselves off from new information, we'll never really be sure of anything. Until we are willing to question the validity of our long-held beliefs, we'll continue to flounder in the dark, easily manipulated into doing the bidding of others.

Like most kids of my generation, I grew up watching School House Rock on TV and can still recite every patriotic song from those videos; in fact, it's what helped me seamlessly recite the Preamble on a dime – to my Drill Sergeant's chagrin – when I was randomly called on to do so during Army Basic Training (thanks ABC!). But School House Rock wasn't my first brush with patriotism; that distinction goes to my mom. My mom is one of the most courageous people I know, and by far the greatest U.S. patriot I've ever met – and I've met many. A pregnant 22-year-old newlywed, she emigrated to the U.S. from Cuba with her mother, leaving her family, friends, and young husband (my dad) behind (at his insistence) when her Visa was suddenly approved after seven years of waiting. The full breadth of the Castro regime's destructive policies had begun to reveal themselves, and the writing was on the wall; there was no way that either of my parents was going to have a child of theirs be born into that chaos if they could help it. I owe every opportunity that's been afforded me since to my mother's selfless act.

My mom is a redheaded firecracker, a sassy debater with no editor when it comes to speaking the truth plainly and vigorously. Having experienced the destruction of

Communism first-hand, she taught my younger sister and me how fortunate we were to be born in this great nation, to take pride in our American History, and to honor the sacrifices made by the countless men and women who fought and died to establish "a more perfect union." She taught us to love our flag and to respect the presidency, and pointed out that if we had the words to criticize the policies of our government then we also had the words to affect change and make a difference; which, although it required a lot more work, was also much more constructive and fulfilling in the end. She taught us not to make excuses – for ourselves or for others – but also, to give people the benefit of the doubt until they proved otherwise. At that point, she taught us never to fear calling things by their rightful name, or speaking truth to power. "That," she assured us, "is your right, your *obligation*, as an American." I daresay she raised us right.

What are my qualifications for writing this book? The same as yours are for reading it: I'm a simple American just like you, who loves her country and is concerned about the welfare of the nation and its People. If there's anything I can do to serve the needs of my country, to aid the team, or to leave things better than I found them, then count me in. I've been a Liberal and I've been a Conservative; I've worked in local politics for years and have been fortunate enough to receive a stellar education – both in the classroom and in life – as to 'the System' and how it works. I do not work for any transnational corporation or bank, nor do I depend on corporate funds for any political campaign. Criticism neither frightens nor deters me; like most outspoken people, I've gotten plenty of it through the years. Just to be clear, my focus is on finding viable, sustainable solutions to the challenges we face as a People, and it trumps any need to be "right" or to "win" any argument. Of course, there are times when I slip up like anyone else and really let somebody have it on the Internet (I can't help it: my mom's a firecracker, remember?); however, I also realize that no solutions will ever be achieved without your cooperation, and keeping this in mind helps me get back on track.

I'm willing to bet that there are enough of you out there who are sick and tired of the spin cycle that U.S. politics has become and who are starting to realize that if anything is going to change, it's going to be up to us to change it. And as humble as our shared qualifications are, I still think they're sufficient to authorize us both in this endeavor moving forward. Thank you for graciously extending me the opportunity to share my insights with you, so that hopefully, they can help us make new strides towards building a better, stronger, and happier America, together.

Politrix

Politrix – n. The art of attaining the improbable, by presenting the impossible, as the inevitable.

"All warfare is based on deception." ~ Sun Tzu

Your representatives are scared of you. They're scared that you will see through the elaborate display of hyper-partisanship that they've concocted since 2001 and see it for what it truly is – political theatre. They're scared that you will peek behind the curtain and realize that there is nothing back there but levers, smoke machines, and a two-way mirror; and that 9 times out of 10, they are working together to advance the interests of their powerful friends in the banking and corporate sectors at your expense. They're afraid that once you stop buying into their narrative, they will lose their audience, their seats, and their power, and that they will have to resort to serving the people's interests – and live up to their promises – if they want to remain in office. Your political awakening will complicate matters and will throw a monkey wrench into an otherwise well-oiled, self-propelled machine, so they'll do and say almost anything to keep you from peeking behind that curtain; and what's worked best for them since time immemorial is exactly what's keeping you from exercising your power – partisanship.

A great deal of writing has been dedicated to the absurd political sniping that has cropped up in America since George W. Bush took office, and which has quickly picked up speed and force after the nomination of Barack Obama; but no one seems to be offering any viable solutions to this phenomenon. "Vote those idiots out of office!" might be a popular response – from all sides of the aisle – but clearly not one that addresses the underlying causes of hyper-partisanship; nor how we can, as a people, do something about it. If we expect anyone in office to change the contentious political atmosphere in Washington and the country at large, we're going to be waiting a long, long time. Why? Because it's in Washington's best interest to keep things going just the way they are, while it's in our best interest that things change. This isn't "cynicism," this is a mere observation founded on common sense and a basic awareness of domestic and foreign policy. If you don't believe me, check out the media ratings of the most partisan news channels and the abundant campaign coffers of the most partisan representatives. Clearly, partisanship is very profitable.

One of the basic purposes of debate and discussion is concession, a reasonable halfway point where most people can agree to meet and from where solutions can be culled. But you can't get to a place of compromise unless you're willing to ask questions and to listen to other points of view. If you ask a guy standing outside a building to describe it from his perspective, you'll get a way different answer than if you ask the guy within the building's second floor supplies closet to do the same; and yet, it's the same building. The only way to get a clearer picture of any structure is to look at it from all angles, both from within and from without; to understand its inner workings, to know even who owns it, what its maintenance costs are, and what revenue it can bring in. The same goes for a nation. In order to fully understand where our country is today, both domestically and within the international community, we have to take a dispassionate look at our economic position and our fiscal policies, as well as our foreign and domestic policies. In a technologically driven, ever-globalized world, the external ramifications of internal actions are immediate and far-reaching. We can either choose our nation's path moving forward, or we can rely on fate to do it for us. I highly recommend the prior.

Some will argue that there is only so much power the American voter has to affect the course of events, that corporate influence has been allowed to flourish to a level in which the people's interests are dwarfed by the hundreds of millions of dollars in lobbying efforts major transnational corporations pour into our political system every year. I won't counter this argument, because I can't; there is enough evidence to support it. However, I pose a different viewpoint. Americans may not enjoy a great deal of power when it comes to their vote, but there are still two potent ways in which we can have our voices heard and our needs addressed – namely, our consumerism, and the court of public opinion.

Put Your Money Where Your Mouth Is...

The most powerful American vote is the one we make each and every day when we spend our money. Even the most influential corporations are at the mercy of this seemingly small action on our part. Capitalism requires a vibrant consumer base in order to function; in other words, if there are no customers, there's no production, and in turn, no profit. Therefore, the power that Americans wield each and every time they swipe their cards to make a purchase is even more effectual than the ballot they cast every two, four, or six years. In this way, we *do* get to dictate corporate policies; why give money to a firm whose business practices are in direct conflict with our interests, or with the welfare of the American people? If the corporations control our elected officials, it is still our consumerism that controls the corporations. Keeping this in mind is Step #1 to turning things around in our favor.

...Then Walk the Talk.

The second most powerful American vote is the one we cast socially, in the court of public opinion. Who hasn't heard of a case in which a murderer is found "not guilty" in a court of law, but guilty as sin in society's eyes? And doesn't society act accordingly, oftentimes making that murderer pay for his or her conduct in a million different (legal) ways? Not to beat a dead horse, but any American who remembers the O.J. Simpson trial can attest to this. Favorable public opinion is essential to any government or regime because it legitimizes it; it's the "stamp of approval" that all political leaders seek in order to assure themselves (and others) that they have the consent of the ruled, in order to keep the peace and conduct business as usual. Without it, governments face a multitude of costly and time-consuming challenges and obstacles, from riots and rebellion within the country – such as the Occupy Wall Street and Tea Party movements in the U.S., as well as the Arab Spring throughout the Middle East – to international pressure through UN involvement if an administration is found to be egregious in its human rights violations or if it's unable to control insurrection and provide for its populace. To quote the great 21st century philosopher Sweet Brown, "Ain't nobody got time for that." Indeed.

But it's not only public figures and governments that require societal acceptance; corporations do too. There are countless examples of how public demand holds business accountable for its policies and pressures industry to act in more responsible ways. For example, the McDonald's Corporation was forced to implement major changes to its menu after Morgan Spurlock's 2004 hit documentary *Super Size Me* educated the masses as to the health risks of eating at the mega-fast food chain; and Mike Wallace's landmark 60 Minutes interview with whistle-blower Jeffrey Wigands in 1996, who gave such a fearless account against Big Tobacco that it spurred a national anti-smoking campaign which has decreased smoking in the U.S. from 24.7% in 1996, to 18.1% in 2012, according to the Center for Disease Control. And the numbers continue to fall. More recently, Eva Longoria plugged her documentary about immigrant farmers in the U.S. – *Food Chains* – on the October 31st, 2014 episode of HBO's *Real Time*, explaining her work promoting the new "Fair Food" label and praising those fast food giants and supermarkets – such as Walmart - that responsibly signed on to assure that their products are provided humanely through a work force that was paid fair wages and ensured safe working conditions; but more importantly, she acknowledged that two giants of the food industry – Publix Supermarkets in Florida, and Wendy's national fast food joint – still refused to sign onto the initiative. Bill Maher has almost 3 million followers on Twitter alone; if these folks were inspired to demand it, it's conceivable that they'd easily have the consumer power to change Publix and Wendy's mind about what constitutes responsible corporate policy. The court of public opinion has and does affect policy and corporate behavior: keeping this in mind is Step #2 to turning things around in our favor.

These are the people's tools: by using our dollars wisely and by vociferously bringing the issues that matter to light through social media as well as social activism (yes, this means getting off your sofa and doing something more than just retweeting and clicking "Like" on Facebook), the American voter, the American tax payer, still wields a considerable amount of power in the United States and the world. So what's stopping us?

The biggest challenge we face in exercising that power stems from our inability to gel our efforts and clearly define our goals as a People; we have sacrificed a great deal of our influence squabbling amongst ourselves and calling each other names, instead of focusing on defining what our collective goals are and what steps we need to take to achieve them. Hyper-partisanship and the fear-mongering that almost always accompanies it are nothing more than a ruse, a distraction aimed at scattering our focus away from delving behind the real threats we face as a nation, to blaming each other over absurd non-issues that only serve to spark endless online debates, but that do nothing to solve our collective problems. Ask yourself honestly how much more of this diversion the American people can afford to entertain.

Emotionally satisfying as it may be to "win" a FaceBook or Twitter debate, to "annihilate" our opponent with a witticism or factoid fired to obliterate our "adversary's" argument, does it get us any closer to our political goals?

Do you even know what your political goals *are?* Are they constructive, efforts you can be proud to sign your name to; or are you just wasting everyone's time venting, including your own? Are you voluntarily and unconsciously surrendering the only political power you really have? Flinging insults is counterproductive because it closes people's minds against your message and prevents you from getting your point of view heard where it matters most, which is another purpose of debate and discussion. It's like opening a restaurant and using mockery and sarcasm as a marketing tactic; no matter how delicious your food is, if you marginalize your potential customers, if you make them doubt the sincerity of your efforts, you'll be eating that food all by yourself. If your arguments are truly solid, if your ideas honestly serve and benefit others, then why not present them in a way that will get more people to consider them, even buy into them?

Americans need a basic foundation for constructive debate that will get more of us on the same page. Why? Because it's in our best interest as a people to do so. Keep in mind, however, that an independent thinking and independent voting populace is a frightening thought for those who profit from the mirage of the "two-party system." Clearly there are interests that will resist the ideas in this book by all means necessary because, quite frankly, it benefits them that we continue to fight amongst ourselves and ignore what they're up to while we're doing so; because partisanship keeps politicians in office no matter how incompetent they are, or how corrupt, or how destructive their policies.

Keep in mind the reasons why you take the time to be politically involved to begin with – because you believe in the principles your nation was founded on, because you care about your family and the future of the nation, and want to contribute to its success. Keep in mind what your goals are – hopefully, to create solutions and amass the support required to create change where it's needed. Not to "win" arguments on social media. Not to toe the line, for anyone.

In the following chapters, I offer seven simple "rules of engagement" with specific steps and tools that will help you achieve your goals and cut through the BS, nurturing an environment where you can start creating and implementing solid solutions. Here's an overview:

1. **Drop your labels.** Judge candidates as individuals, on their associations, and on the repercussions of their voting records - not on whether they have a "D" or an "R" after their name. If it's a new candidate without much of a voting record, then stick to the soundness of their platform and where you think it will succeed or fail; and to those they associate with, especially their campaign contributors. And don't confuse those who share your interests with the political parties that claim to represent you; only your fellow American is on your same team. Wise up.

2. **Ask questions (and listen to the answers).** Don't assume that you know what the response will be. Give others the benefit of the doubt and ask them where they stand on the issues, and most importantly, why. You might learn something.

3. **Share the facts.** We're all entitled to our opinions, but they should be based on solid data, not emotional reactions to events, or to prejudices that stem from handed-down fears and misconceptions. That being

said, facts aren't missiles to be hurled against those on our own team; share them, don't fire them. There's a big difference.

4. **Play fair.** There is no way to reach logical conclusions when your perceptions are based on faulty reasoning. Avoid using fallacies in your argument – they only create confusion and discord, alienating your opponent, and distracting from the subject at hand. You may be tempted to use them to sway a crowd in your favor, but if you become known for these tactics, you will destroy your own credibility.

5. **Change your mind.** When we get new information, it's normal to adjust our viewpoint to reflect the facts; don't shy away from this. You are under no obligation to hold the same opinions today that you held when you were 18 years old; likewise, you're free to change your mind tomorrow as well. Don't forget to extend this flexibility to others.

6. **Switch sides.** Shifting your perspective gives you insight, and helps you highlight how your points serve the needs of those you are addressing. If your argument is truly valid, you should be able to explain how it benefits those who may have disagreed with you initially. The ability to see the issues from others' point of view will help you see the flaws in your position and to either adjust it, or abandon it altogether in favor of a more productive stance.

7. **Play nice.** No personal attacks. This should go without saying, but unfortunately, it happens way too often. If you have a valid point, make it. If your ideas are challenged, don't panic; be grateful for the opportunity to clarify your point of view to a broader audience. Expletives and name-calling aren't going to help you get your point across. In this digital age, all data can be saved and used against you in the future; don't say anything that you'll regret later on.

If you follow these simple rules, I promise you'll see a major improvement in your political discourse; you may even surprise yourself and come up with new initiatives that will gain in popularity and that you can then confidently present to your local government and federal representatives for implementation. We get the government we show up for. By consolidating our efforts and working together - instead of against each other - we have a better chance of getting a government that will work for the benefit of the American People. And that's a government we all can believe in.

Let's begin.

Basic Concepts I: The Actors

"Know thyself." ~ Chilon of Sparta

First things, first. In order to appreciate the following chapters, it's important to understand how the domestic polity of the United States is broken down here, and what one of our most powerful national precepts – the Free Market – actually is.

The Actors

There are three major players involved in American Realpolitik:

1. The Government
2. The Corporations (Industry)
3. The People

There is a fourth, the Banks, which control the currency values, interest rates, and ultimately, the debt ratios of all nations; needless to say, the power of the Banks is extensive and has broad implications in regards to a nation's political, economic, and social climate. But the actions of this actor are so complicated and so far afield the scope of this work that exploring them here would be like delving into the behavior of the engineers of a stadium in a book about the athletes that perform within it. I encourage you to do the research on your own about this player; it will help you make better sense of our domestic as well as our foreign policy.

Like three legs of one stool, each actor is necessary and provides valuable functions to a productive and civilized society. For example, the People need Government in order to provide the protections necessary to create an environment conducive to freedom. Think about it – if you're constantly fighting off aggressors (either foreign or domestic), you aren't really free to write the next great American novel or to discover the cure for cancer, are you? In addition, the People need Industry to provide the goods and services that free up their time and allow them to achieve their highest potential in their respective fields. For example, if you're forced to cobble your own shoes, sew your own clothes, and grow your own food, when, exactly, would you have the time to do anything else? The products and services created by Industry are what allows us to do more with less; it was the invention of the light bulb and its mass production that allowed other inventors to stay up through the night working on their ideas; it was the boat, the automobile, and the airplane that facilitated travel and expanded our horizons and our reach – both social and economic; and it was the computer that brought the entire world closer together, without even stepping a foot outside of our own homes. In countless ways, both the Government and Industry provide invaluable functions for the Individual by creating an environment in which the Individual is truly "free" to progress.

Likewise, both the Government and Industry depend on the Individual – to labor, to innovate, to consume the goods and services that keep our economy thriving, and to pull together as one society for the advancement of the nation on the world stage. American products are easier to export when the American People are perceived as thriving and happy, when American culture is desirable; American policies are easier to spread abroad when foreign populations admire our lifestyle and demand similar policies from their own governments. The happier the American People are, the easier it is for both Government and Industry to meet their own goals.

However, it's important to note that these three actors have vastly different agendas. Sometimes they collide; sometimes, they compliment each other and coalesce. The needs of the Government and the Corporations tend to overlap more often then the needs of the Government and the People, or the People and the Corporations; but neither the Government nor the Corporations can afford to have a populace that questions the status quo, which is why you're rarely reminded that your side isn't necessarily *their* side. Many folks have bought into the idea that either the Government or the Corporations have the People's best interests in mind, and that if either were left to function unregulated and uncontained, they would naturally benefit the People through "mutual interests," but nothing could be further from the truth. Only the People can have the People's best interests in mind, and only the People are incentivized to promote their own welfare. On the other hand, each actor requires support from the other two, which is the glue that keeps the legs attached to the stool and keeps society functioning.

Most people look out for the interests of their own "team," and that includes the elites that work in the Government and Corporate sectors. But unlike the Government and Corporate sectors, who consolidate their efforts for profit and gain, the People have somehow been convinced to divide themselves into ever smaller groups that do nothing but fight against one another. If the People are going to protect their stakes, this divisiveness has to stop. Self-interest is the driver behind the behavior of each of the three actors, but self-interest isn't inherently good, bad, right, or wrong; it just *is*. Understanding this and accepting it will help us act in ways that are more conducive to meeting our own needs.

1. The Government

What the Government needs from the People are their votes and the legitimacy that their votes afford the political structure; what it needs from the Corporations is money and innovation. Now I'm not referring to sundry paper-pushers who make up the bulk of our massive bureaucracies here, but to the millionaires and billionaires that sit in the highest offices of Government, and who have the ability to create law and control foreign and domestic policy.

In our system of government – a Republic "by the people, for the people" – consent of the ruled is paramount to the elected officials that wield power because it validates their position both domestically and in the international community at large. In order to function efficiently, the Government needs the People to "buy in" to the system. If the People stopped voting, if the People ceased political involvement, if the People stopped lending their consent to be ruled, it would signal a dangerous precedent that could develop into full-fledged public dissent and chaos. This scenario wouldn't serve anyone, least of all the Government. In order to keep everyone involved and active, our Government has cleverly marketed itself as two "different" parties, creating an illusion of rivalry and choice that keeps the masses entangled in political discourse, arguing incessantly against one another, and, more importantly, voting.

Our Founding Fathers warned us against the "two-party" system, as they were pretty smart guys and knew all the tricks of the trade. In a letter to Jonathan Jackson on October 2, 1780, John Adams wrote:

> There is nothing with I dread so much as a division of the republic into two great parties, each arranged under its leader, and concerting measures in opposition to each other. This, in my humble apprehension, is to be dreaded as the greatest political evil under our Constitution.

In his farewell speech in 1796, President George Washington expressed similar concerns with political parties, citing that although these false rivalries might work to inspire patriotism in *"Governments of a Monarchical cast,"* they had the opposite effect in elective-type governments, such as our own:

> There is an opinion, that parties in free countries are useful checks upon the administration of the Government, and serve to keep alive the spirit of Liberty. This within certain limits is probably true; and in Governments of a Monarchical cast, Patriotism may look with indulgence, if not with favor, upon the spirit of party. But in those of the popular character, in Governments purely elective,

it is a spirit not to be encouraged. From their natural tendency, it is certain there will always be enough of that spirit for every salutary purpose. And, there being constant danger of excess, the effort ought to be, by force of public opinion, to mitigate and assuage it. A fire not to be quenched, it demands a uniform vigilance to prevent its bursting into a flame, lest, instead of warming, it should consume.

Never has this been truer in the United States than today, where, as of November 2014, Congress held an abysmal 14% approval rating. Surprisingly, Congressional incumbents held a 95% reelection rate, which boggles the mind. You would think that a voting populace dissatisfied with the performance of their elected officials would have the good sense to vote them out, but this absurd contradiction is the natural result of the "two-party" system, which protects incumbents from competition from within their own party and instead pits one ideology against another, rather than comparing the merits of each candidate individually. It's slim pickens for voters, who are really only presented with two candidates from which to choose (voting for anyone else is considering "throwing your vote away"); and even if a voter doesn't like the incumbent, they will most likely continue to vote for him or her if it means keeping the "other" party out of power – sadly, even if it means ineffective leadership, or worse, leadership that is actively voting against its constituents' best interests. In this way, the People effectively incentivize extremism and poor performance in their elected officials, who realized long ago that in order to get votes all they have to do is tell the people what they want to hear, and keep up the "Us vs. Them" illusion.

The "two-party" system works the same way that sports do, and produces the same kind of inebriating passion; but in politics, you don't even get real competition like you would in athletics, and there is no level playing field. There is no regular season where any number of teams are allowed to compete; there are no "Conferences" or "Divisional Rounds" from which the best teams are culled to compete for a spot in the political Superbowl; no. There are only two teams that monopolize our entire political system, and by and large the winning team isn't chosen by how well it actually performs, but by how much money it can amass. Because of this, the two major parties – through the sheer magnitude of their numbers – are able to swallow the bulk of campaign contributions and successfully keep all other parties from playing, compelling candidates to choose a team if they're going to have a snowball's chance of running a successful campaign. Whatever party makes the most in contributions has the resources to bombard the voting bloc with its message and, the public being what it is, this usually translates into a win.

Solution #1: Top Two Open Primaries

One way to counter this is by holding Top Two Open Primaries (TTOP), in which all eligible candidates are placed on a single ballot, and where all voters are given the opportunity to vote for the candidate they feel best represents them regardless of the candidate's or the voter's party affiliation. The candidates with the top two highest votes go on to compete in the general election; and no, incumbents are not protected from competition from within their own parties. Top Two Open Primaries ensure that Non-Party Affiliation (NPA), minor, and Independent candidates and voters are able to participate in primaries, as opposed to having to register with a major party in order to run or vote. Both California and Washington State run Top Two Open Primaries successfully, and groups such as NoLables.org and IndependentVoting.org are resolutely working towards expanding this platform in order to get better representation for those American voters who prefer to focus on common-sense, common-ground ideas and problem-solving, instead of on partisan divisions and contention. According to Ray Hudkins of Florida Fair and Open Primaries, over 2.9 million NPA, minor party, and independent voters are shut out of Florida's closed primaries; they pay for primary elections but can't participate in them – a clear violation of their individual and collective rights, a great example of "taxation without representation."

With TTOPs, parties would still hold meetings, caucuses, and conventions to select candidates that would run for election in the primary; however, they would not be guaranteed a place on the general election ballot, as it's an open race. It's useful to keep in mind that school boards, the judiciary races, and some municipalities already hold viable nonpartisan races. Of course, there is great opposition to TTOPs, as it would put control of the election squarely in the hands of the voters and away from political parties; but the arguments against TTOPs don't hold water when tested.

For example, disputants argue that TTOPs will encourage a ground swell of single party candidates (Republican vs. Republican, or Democrat vs. Democrat), but this hasn't been the case in Washington State, California, or Louisiana, all states that hold Top Two Open, or "blanket," primaries.

Another argument is that there will be a lot of "cross over voting," where the members of one party will vote for the weakest member of the opposing party in order to stack the odds in favor of their favorite candidate; but this argument lacks logic. Because all candidates are on a single ballot, voters get just one vote. And because incumbents have to compete just like every other eligible candidate, voting for a weak candidate as a strategy to protect an incumbent won't work.

A third opposition argument is that TTOPs have low voter turnout, but – surprise, surprise – that's true of all primaries across the board; not just because the exhaustive process running up to the primaries tends to attract only the most hard-core politicos out there, but because by and large the voting bloc is dissatisfied with the choices they're presented with. The purpose of Top Two Open Primaries isn't necessarily to increase voter turnout, which may definitely end up being a secondary effect, but to get more voters engaged in the voting process. Of course, the major parties feel that they are entitled to have control over the primaries, so they'd rather keep them closed, and they'll do and say almost anything to keep them that way, thank you very much.

Solution #2: Term Limits

Another great way to counter an inefficient Government system is to implement term limits on its officers. Public office was meant to be a temporary service for the People, not a life-long career; but today, public office and the many perks that come along with it (lobbying kickbacks, book deals, insider stock market info, profitable connections in the private sector, and lucrative speaker fees at large and private gatherings, etc.) have become the main source of income for many politicians. Because this is the case, too many politicians are willing to do whatever it takes to remain in office. And while small donors make for great press, no politician gets elected without major donors. In fact, according to OpenSecrets.org, even in the contentious 2008 Presidential Election, little over one-half of one percent of Americans gave more than $200 to any federal candidate, party, or PAC. Which brings me to the third way to counter Government waste and corruption – get Corporate money out of our political system.

Solution #3: Campaign Reform

Countless millions of dollars are spent on manipulating political campaigns, and that number has only swelled since the Supreme Court's 2010 ruling in the Citizens United case. Money has now been labeled "speech," and Corporations are now "people," free to pump as much money as they wish into the coffers of their favorite team, for the political party that best represents their interests (or more commonly, they hedge their bets and give generously to both parties, "just in case") without disclosure; not directly, but indirectly to a party or candidate's Super PAC. But directly or indirectly, what difference does it make? The results are exactly the same. It doesn't take a genius to figure out how this has affected our political system: in order to attract vital Corporate money, Corporate interests now take priority in our Government, regardless of which party is in power. When money is speech, only the wealthy have a voice.

It astounds me when I hear Americans claim that you "can't trust the Government because it's corrupt," but then turn around and advocate that Industry *can* be trusted – even though it's Industry that's doing all of the Government corrupting. Where is the logic here? I've heard too many

Americans complain that they're opposed to what they see as a Government that lends itself to bribery, nepotism, and overall crookedness, but then when regulations are proposed to keep Industry from having the power to leverage our elected leaders, these same people fly to the defense of Industry's "right" to do just that, calling it "freedom." Cheerleading for Industry's influence on Government and simultaneously complaining about it is irrational; first of all, we can't have it both ways – either buying influence in Government is wrong, or it isn't. Secondly, nowhere did our Founding Fathers advocate that "freedom" meant allowing Industry to bargain its way into the halls of Government, but they did warn us *against* it repeatedly.

The Government is supposed to act as a referee between Public and Private interests, ensuring that all actors play according to the rules and that each are equally able to promote their agenda so long as doing so doesn't deny the other actor from doing the same. But today, the Government has become a referee that consistently and unfairly sides with one actor over the other. That doesn't mean that we should get rid of referees altogether – because obviously, getting rid of oversight isn't going to make unethical players any more honest – only that corrupt referees need to be removed and replaced with those who are better able to fulfill their obligations. The same goes for our Government: in order to create a more legitimate system, we need to get our representatives off the Corporate payroll by repealing the laws that allow Industry to purchase our lawmakers. Buying Government influence isn't "freedom," it's coercive, deceptive, and fraudulent. When it comes to restraining the power of Corporate money in politics, we're either part of the solution, or we're part of the problem. As the People learn to rely less on rhetoric and labels, and more on facts and consequences, we'll be better able to discern which policies work in our interests, and which are actually working against us.

Reform in Action

Unbeknownst to many Americans, the Securities Exchange Commission (SEC) has the ability to issue a rule requiring publicly traded corporations to disclose their political contributions; in 2014, a petition was submitted to the SEC that was crafted by ten experts in corporate and securities law calling for the agency to compel publicly traded companies to disclose their political spending. However, the SEC has all but ignored it, compelling Campaign for Accountability to sue the SEC on behalf of investor Stephen Silberstein in order to get the SEC to fulfill its obligations and do what it legally can to ensure a more transparent political system. Americans interested in campaign reform can petition the SEC through either Public Citizen or Common Cause, both members of the Corporate Reform Coalition; a quick Google search will put you in contact with these groups.

Represent.us, a left-right coalition, is also working on creating limits on lobbying, political donations, and PACs and Super PACs. Self-described as a "special sauce of brains and brawn who really don't like corruption," these representatives are petitioning to get a million Americans to support their bill before they introduce it, and they're asking every member of the House to go on the record either for or against the American Anti-Corruption Act, giving the People full disclosure on where their representatives stand on this vital issue.

Other organizations aim to make campaign finance reform a central issue of the upcoming 2016 presidential election cycle; for example, Rootstrikers in New Hampshire are organizing walkathons across the country to bring this issue to the fore, as well as by repeatedly asking all candidates the one vital question: "How will YOU end the system of corruption in Washington?" (Visit NHRebellion.org to find out more).

There are many ways in which the People can and should coordinate their efforts in order to ensure that the Government fulfills its obligations without overstepping its boundaries and without sacrificing the interests of the People in favor of those of the Corporations – which, clearly, are not the same.

2. The Corporations (Industry)

What the Corporations need from the People are their money (consumerism), their labor, their innovation, and their willingness to vote for candidates that will promote Corporate interests; what they need from the Government are domestic laws and international treaties that will allow them to operate under the radar and free from the regulations that impede their ability to amass the greatest profit possible. Also, they need the Government's resources to enforce those laws and treaties, which oftentimes translates into military action.

Again, to be clear, I am not talking about small "Mom & Pop" outfits that make less than $5 million annually; I'm talking about huge, multi-national corporations that have the monetary resources to affect entire economies world-wide, including our own; and who use their resources to affect political systems internationally and here at home.

Every time I bring up Corporations I get a slew of small business owners hurling insults at me and decrying the Government regulations and taxes that often offset any profit they make after the risks and efforts they take each and every day. Although small businesses employ roughly 52% of the American labor pool, outside of the Small Business Administration, they do not carry the political weight that the large transnational Corporations do. Again, I am not referring to small businesses here, and I apologize for any confusion I may have caused by not making this distinction earlier.

Depending on how they predict their constituents will react, elected officials may or may not admit that they will, in fact, work in conjunction with their peers in Congress and elsewhere to create policies that will benefit the Corporations; but you can always find out where their priorities really lie by looking up their voting records and who their campaign contributors are. This is all public knowledge, and there is no end to legitimate websites that will provide this information to anyone willing to do the research. Although Super PACs have been able to effectively veil Corporate political contributions, where there's a will, there's a way; it's really difficult to keep this information completely hidden in the digital age. If you follow the money, you will get a clearer picture of where a candidate truly stands, whom their allies really are, and why. You might also be able to predict whom the Corporate winners and losers will be in the coming years. Follow the money and look at what they do, instead of what they tell you they'll do.

Any student of American economic history, especially that of the 20th century, can attest that there is a connection between our involvement in armed conflict and Corporate interests; the Dulles brothers are a prime example of this American paradigm. John Foster Dulles served as the U.S. Secretary of State from 1953 to 1959 under President Dwight D. Eisenhower, at the same time that his brother, Allen Welsh Dulles, served as Director of the CIA; together, these men crafted a series of foreign military exploits that eventually brought the United States into a Cold War with the Soviet Union and into the Vietnam War, causing far-reaching, world-wide repercussions we are dealing with to this very day. One of the most famous events the Dulles brothers concocted was the CIA-backed coup d'état that deposed the democratically elected Guatemalan President, Colonel Jacobo Árbenz Guzmán, ostensibly in an effort to combat "communism" but in reality to protect the interests of their Corporate friends.

Upon his election in 1951, Guzman began to implement socially beneficial policies such as the expansion of suffrage and broader access to education. His pet policy however, was agrarian reform, which would grant fertile lands to the poverty-stricken peasant class in his country and that would end the system of debt peonage. Unfortunately for Guzman, this policy directly conflicted with the investments of the United Fruit Company (UFCO), an American firm that claimed ownership of the lands and kept them uncultivated in order to drive up the price of their produce, mainly bananas. The UFCO lobbied the U.S. government; the result was the violent overthrow of Guzman, courtesy of the American military and the American taxpayers, and a string of Guatemalan dictators put and kept in power by Uncle Sam – including the genocidal Efrain Rios Montt, who put hundreds of Mayans to death in the 80s with the support of President Ronald Reagan. Consequently, we have a decimated Guatemala that for years has served as a distribution route for South American drug cartels into the U.S.

Not since *War is a Racket,* the booklet and speech written in 1935 by retired U.S. Marine Corps Major General and two-time Medal of Honor recipient, Smedley D. Butler, have the People – and the world – been afforded such a brutally honest look into the drivers behind American foreign policy and the politics behind war profiteering. As difficult as General Butler's commentary is to accept for many Americans today, it is even more difficult to ignore and impossible to discount.

> War is a racket. It always has been. It is possibly the oldest, easily the most profitable, surely the most vicious. It is the only one international in scope. It is the only one in which the profits are reckoned in dollars and the losses in lives. A racket is best described, I believe, as something that is not what it seems to the majority of the people. Only a small 'inside' group knows what it is about. It is conducted for the benefit of the very few, at the expense of the very many. Out of war a few people make huge fortunes.

He then goes on to propose three concrete steps to curb the "war racket." I highly recommend that you take the time to read his brief but powerful work for yourself, especially if you are a member of the military or if you have any loved ones that serve.

I use these examples because these events happened long enough ago to afford us the luxury of retrospect, not because these practices have ceased to exist. If you want to know how Corporate interests continue to shape our Government and our military involvement around the world today, simply follow the money. Which companies have profited from our involvement in war? How much have these companies invested in political campaigns, and to whom? It's really that simple.

3. The People

"The People" are everyone else, those of us who don't directly control policy, law making, or the economy. What the People need from the Government is the protection of our national and state borders, adherence to the U.S. Constitution and our civil rights and liberties contained therein, and the protection of our property, which includes the protection of our shared public goods and national reserves such as our labor pool and our natural resources – air, water, and land; and also, the protection of our national welfare over private interests, which includes our economy and our social and political structures. We do not need the Government to micro-manage our lives. We do not need the Government to strip us of our rights and liberties in the name of "security." We do not need the Government to use our national resources to promote the agendas of private entities at our own expense.

What the People need from the Corporations is innovation, supply to adequately meet demand, fair wages and safe working conditions in exchange for their labor, and an honest exchange of goods and services for mutual gain. We do not need the Corporations to get involved in policy-making, to define states craft, or to monopolize industry therefore diminishing our choices in the marketplace as consumers, as well as limiting our own ability to innovate and enter the market as producers.

What the People need from *each other* has been too long forgotten, if it was ever sufficiently addressed; and it's vital to ensuring that our own shared interests are promoted and protected: a commitment to one another and to the promotion and protection of our shared interests; a readiness to conduct due diligence – to understand at least the basics of economics, foreign policy, domestic issues, and scientific discovery as it pertains to our resources – and to accept the facts that frame them; civic responsibility, including not just voting but also educating ourselves and others about current issues; honest discourse and respectful debate so that we can figure out how to move forward; a willingness to unify our efforts to come up with solutions to the challenges we face together; and shared efforts to get them implemented.

Because I am writing this book for you – the People – and not for the Government nor for the Corporations, it is imperative that you accept that these three players are separate actors, and that neither the Government nor the Corporations will inherently look out for your best interests. It's been popular for a while now to "choose a side" and believe that either bigger Government or the "Free Market" (unregulated Corporations) would best serve the needs of the People, but this is a fallacy; only the People will serve the needs of the People. There is no point in making comparisons between two actors that both seek out their own gain, in order judge which is the lesser of two evils; it's an exercise in futility. The People can't afford that luxury.

Keep in mind that the Government would expand its powers indefinitely if it were able; the Government is not in the business of upholding the notion of a Constitutional Republic that, by definition, reigns in Government's power. There's a lot of money to be made in Government, and as the saying goes, "It's good to be King." Likewise, Industry would expand its powers ceaselessly if it could; Corporations are not in the business of upholding the notion of a "Free Market" that by definition reigns in Corporate profit and forces them to compete for revenue. The corporations with resources large enough to control the markets completely would like nothing more than to do exactly that. history has proven this time and time again. It's just the nature of the beast.

We, the People, must keep these actors and their attributes clearly in mind whenever we are acting politically. I am not advocating an end to Government or an end to Industry; I've already stated that every player has value and our high standard of living depends on each player doing its part. But in order for this system to work and not implode upon itself, all three players must act responsibly and a balance of power and interests must be maintained.

It's all good and well to prefer one candidate over the others, to support the campaigns and platforms of elected officials that we see are honestly making sound policy decisions *when* they make them; however, as the People, we must never forget that at the end of the day, they are still politicians – and politicians require our objective oversight to keep them honest. Blind faith has no place in our political system in any form, or in our political stance as voters.

A Word to the Wise

Some will argue that regulations restrict "freedom" and are un-American, fundamentally going against our founding principles; but outside of the freedom of speech – the right to free expression, the most basic human right on par with the right to self-defense – the definition of "freedom" has been systemically stretched to absurd limits, transformed into an inchoate, amorphous term that can be molded to fit the needs of any argument. In order to avoid a snow job, we need to understand how freedom is being defined when it's conjured up in a debate, and more specifically, *who* is defining it. You see, the way in which words are defined – the meaning that is attached to them – is a very powerful tool in the art of manipulation. The definition words are given shapes the way situations are interpreted and how people are characterized; it controls public opinion to serve the needs of whoever is constructing the meaning. For example, "terrorists" are also defined as "freedom fighters," depending on whom you ask. The difference in definition doesn't change the acts of these groups one bit, but it does affect the way that these people are perceived, and whether they will garner support from others – either through clandestine funding or recruitment – or if they will inspire entire nations to rally against them and their efforts through war and domestic surveillance tactics. The way "tolerance" is defined can mislead even the most compassionate people to support ideologies and practices that are not only barbaric, regressive, murderous, and oppressive, but which actively work against the very tenets of democracy and equality that "tolerance" is supposed to promote. The term "freedom" is no different, and can and has been used to excuse many questionable policies of and permissions allowed to Industry.

Unless we take a minute to understand the interests of the definer, and what they stand to gain by their definitions; unless we are able to question whether or not the definitions we are being fed coalesce with our own understanding of what those words mean, we can easily be led to support policies and ideas that actually work against us. If we choose to accept Corporate irresponsibility and avarice as nothing more than the manifestations of "freedom" – a concept whose irrefutable value we've been repeatedly, aggressively, and duplicitously trained to believe is beyond question or examination – our consent will open up a can of worms that no doubt will backfire on the interests of the People and of society as a whole. The question we should be asking ourselves is why would we, the American People, accept, excuse, and even *champion* irresponsibility in Industry when we surely wouldn't accept a lack of accountability from our Government? Why would we rationalize misconduct and the squandering of resources when the charges are attributed to a Corporation, but then quickly and forcefully condemn them in Government? Aren't both equally wrong? And that's not to mention how we react to our fellow Americans when we suspect them of "living off the Government dime"; how can we criticize working Americans who have become dependent on social programs just to make ends meet in a down-turned economy, but then have little complaint against multi-billion dollar bank bailouts, international slave labor, deficient domestic wages, and all sorts of hidden perks collectively called "Corporate Welfare"? After all, aren't Corporations just "people," too? Stop and think for a minute: when the Government claims that protecting you from Corporate predation would "infringe" on your freedoms ... what in the world are they *really* saying?

Sacred Cows are for Sheep

If we're going to understand the forces that shape our perceptions about our economic, social, and political reality, we'll have to begin by mustering up the courage to question everything; nothing – no belief, ideology, rhetoric, or definition – should ever be beyond reproach in a sane and responsible society. That includes reflecting upon the words and concepts that have become sacred to us after generations of unchallenged repetition. Concepts like "freedom." If we intelligently ponder freedom, it becomes clear to us that freedom isn't inherently good or bad; like fire, it simultaneously carries the potential to create *and* to destroy. However, in the U.S., *your* rights and your freedom end where *mine* begin. License to pollute the air, water, and soil wouldn't serve the nation; neither would the freedom to murder at will, or to create law arbitrarily. We have restrictions for a reason, and checks and balances ensure that the interests of one actor aren't fulfilled at the expense of the others. For fire to serve the needs of a productive and civilized society, it has to be used judiciously and responsibly, taking into account both its creative and destructive properties; likewise for freedom. Why? Because rights and obligations go hand-in-hand, you can't rationally have one without the other. To grant rights and freedoms without defining and enforcing commensurate obligations is a recipe for disaster. Any parent can attest to this, but also, a quick review of history will reveal the same.

Contrary to popular belief, checks and balances don't just protect the People from an overbearing Government, but from rapacious Industrial drivers as well; again, each of these other two actors have distinct agendas which they don't share with you, the People, and which they actively seek to advance in any (legal?) way possible. Your interests as the People are your own responsibility to define and defend; don't look to the other two actors to do it for you unless they are compelled to do so. Luckily, at least in the United States, you've been given the tools to promote your welfare and preserve your rights – consumerism, the court of public opinion, and of course, the Constitution. Use them.

A Word About Taxes

Theft occurs when something is taken from you with nothing in return; taxes do not fall into this category, unless your taxes are being used *against* you instead of *for* you. Taxes are not theft when they fund clean water and streets, safe roads, effective schools, a sanitation department, public health services, the conservation of public spaces such as parks and natural resources, public safety services such as responsible and dependable police and fire departments, emergency services, etc. Taxes become theft when they are used to fund questionable wars that primarily benefit the munitions, weapons, and oil Industries; when they are used to subsidize the labor expenses of behemoth Corporations; and when they are used to "bail out" predatory Banks and their reckless business models.

The American middle class today is shrinking because the wealthiest Americans are able to influence tax laws that allow them to pay miniscule returns for the great benefits they receive living and producing in America. I've heard people say, "Great! That means that they won't be funding our Government's insatiable lust for war!" But unfortunately, that's not how it works. When the top .01% of Americans pays fewer taxes, then the middle class pays more; and it's the public services that *we* need – such as our school programs, our clean water programs, our police and fire departments – that get budget cuts. War never gets a cut; it will always be funded as long as there is profit to be made. The question is, who pays for it, and who benefits?

Most economic textbooks will assure you that when Industry is allowed to pay fewer taxes, it takes the savings and reinvests it, creating jobs; but while that may have been how business was conducted *before* the advent of NAFTA, that's just not true anymore. Many large Corporations make their profits from playing the market; hiring American workers isn't profitable anymore, not when they can go to Cambodia or Bangladesh and get labor for slave wages. So just what *do* Corporations do with the money they get to keep?

Because of our convoluted tax laws, Corporations are allowed to keep huge amounts of their revenue offshore without being taxed, as long as they never bring the money back into the U.S. This causes two things to happen: 1. Corporations aren't able to use large chunks of cash they have sitting in foreign banks and therefore 2. Corporations borrow money they don't have and then offset the interest of these loans by deducting them and paying even *fewer* taxes in America, which further drives down the nation's tax revenues. In 2004, Bill HR 4520 passed, which allowed Corporations to repatriate cash at a mere 5% tax rate. George Bush proposed that the bill was a "job creating" tax holiday that would end up stimulating the American economy. Instead, Pfizer repatriated $11 billion and the minute they got the money back into the U.S., they fired thousands of workers and used the money to buy back their own stocks, driving up the value of the stocks for their investors and executives; Merck repatriated $15.9 billion from 2004-2005, and cut 7,000 jobs; Ford repatriated $900 million from 2004-2005, and closed 10 plants in North America, with a plan to eliminate 25-30,000 jobs in the following five years; and Citigroup repatriated $3.2 billion from 2004-2005, and celebrated by cutting 17,000 jobs in 2007. So much for the "job creating" effects of giving tax breaks to Corporations.

Who allowed Industry these tax breaks? Their friends in the Government, of course. It's silly for the People to argue the merits of the Government vs. the merits of Big Business, because they work in tandem for gain. They aren't on opposing teams; on the contrary, some have argued that in today's America, they've become one and the same – literally one entity. So…why do *we* insist on dividing ourselves?

What about the Military?

I get this question a lot. Those who serve in the military are by and large culled from the People, but oftentimes – as history has already shown – they end up serving the interests of the Corporations at the command of the Government; this puts the Military in a strange position, because whether or not Industry gains from military force, it is the Government that pays for that force through taxation. Although the first vow taken by all Military members is to "support and defend the Constitution of the United States against all enemies, foreign and domestic," they serve under the orders of the Commander in Chief, an officer of the Government. Therefore, for the sake of the practical application of the ideas in this book, the Military falls under the purview of the Government.

Basic Concepts II:
The Free Market

"Consumption is the sole end and purpose of all production; and the interest of the producer ought to be attended to only so far as it may be necessary for promoting that of the consumer."
~ Adam Smith, *The Wealth of Nations*

The Free Market

It's important here to define the "Free Market" because most people who fling this term around don't seem to fully understand that there actually *are* rules and requirements to this concept. "Free Market" doesn't mean you get to produce goods and services by any means necessary – theft, pollution, or the exploitation of underpaid labor. It's not a "free for all" situation where anything goes; it means that you get to sell your goods and services in a market that treats all producers equally, where anyone with a great idea and the capital to develop it is welcome to compete in an unmonopolized market. This distinction has been lost on society at large through years of systemic rhetoric claiming that somehow, "free" means "no holds barred." Nothing could be further from the truth.

When Adam Smith, the father of Capitalism and modern economics, wrote *An Inquiry into the Nature and Causes of the Wealth of Nations* in 1776, he defined the conditions for a system that would enable the most productive economy and which would act in the "public interest," laying the foundations of the classical free market economic theory that we use today. Smith believed that the rational self-interest of and competition amongst producers would lead to economic prosperity, and he trusted that Industry's drive for profit would naturally benefit the public welfare like an "invisible hand," because self-interest would compel firms to produce better goods at cheaper prices in order to gain the greatest amount of customers, directing "industry in such a manner as its produce may be of the greatest value."

However, he also warned against the threat of monopolies and collusion between private firms who work together to increase prices in order to maximize their profit at the expense of the consumer. He pointed out that Government subsidies and protections would only create inefficiencies in production, which are especially threatening when Industry is allowed to dominate the political system, cautioning that:

> The proposal of any new law or regulation of commerce which comes from this order (industry), ought always to be listened to with great precaution, and ought never be adopted till after having been long and carefully examined, not only with the most scrupulous, but with the most suspicious attention.

Does this even remotely resemble the United States today? Industry today has not only been elevated to the state of "personhood," but is allowed a seat at the table when foreign and domestic policies are crafted. That's nuts.

Adam Smith proposed that value was a product of labor (the "Labor Theory of Value"), and his writings supported a minimum wage and a higher tax rate for the wealthiest citizens, pointing out that the more one gets out of a system, the more one is obliged to pay into it:

> It is not very unreasonable that the rich should contribute to the public expense, not only in proportion to their revenue, but something more than in that proportion.

For a nation that prides itself as a Capitalist State, it seems that America has forgotten the basic foundations of true Capitalism.

Wages and Inflation

Few Americans today realize that the ideology of "fair wages" isn't in conflict with Capitalism but is actually one of its founding principles, because once the Labor Theory of Value became central to Marxism, it was vilified and discounted as being "anti-business." But is it? Doesn't commerce require productive and skilled labor not only to create valuable goods, but also to provide consumers? After all, where does Industry get its consumers if not from a sufficiently employed labor pool that can not only afford goods but that also has a need for a greater *variety* of goods? Americans who barely make enough to keep a roof over their heads aren't going to have the expendable income to buy extras, but those making good money can, and do.

De-incentivizing work by keeping wages low is counter-productive and creates a citizenry that will demand more and more Socialism; if workers can't get ahead through their own labor, they *will* be forced to turn to the Government to help them survive. You can't expect someone to pull themselves up by their bootstraps if neither the boots nor the straps exist, and you can't blame someone of being irresponsible if the system is already set up in a way that doesn't allow them to get ahead through their own efforts.

A popular misconception that gets repeated a lot is that a higher minimum wage would cause inflation, but in Economics, it's how much money is in *circulation* that affects inflation, not where it's allocated: in other words, the value of any currency depends on how much of that currency *exists*, not on who's holding onto it. For example, let's suppose that there were only 100,000,000 U.S. dollars in existence in America; this would significantly raise the value of the dollar, because it would be scarce. Its high value, however, wouldn't be affected by who holds the 100,000,000 dollars; if one person owned all of the 100,000,000 dollars, or if they were split up evenly amongst the nation's 316.1 million citizens by giving each of them .316355 cents, it wouldn't change the value of the currency, because the amount of dollars wouldn't change. However, if we suddenly printed more dollars, the value *would* change – it would decrease – because now there would be more of them and they would no longer be as scarce. To put it in perspective, if there is only one 56-carat diamond in the world, it would hold more value than if 56-carat diamonds grew on trees (I would probably still want one, however). It's the available amount of anything useful that gives it its worth, and affects its price. This basic principle of economics is the reason why supermarket prices don't shoot up through the roof when the nation's top CEOs make their annual, multi-million dollar bonuses, but they *do* increase when the Federal Reserve practices "Quantitative Easing" and prints up more money out of thin air.

The Fed has ways of trying to soak some of those dollars back up and get them out of circulation in order to keep inflation down, but that topic is far afield the scope of this book. I just want to point out that *where* the money is allocated – *who* is holding it – doesn't affect inflation, so raising the minimum wage wouldn't increase inflation; however, printing more money *can* do that, especially when the velocity of exchange, or how many people are using that money, falls. In Economics, this concept is represented by the equation $MV = Py$, where M = Money supply; V = Velocity (how many times that money exchanges hands); P = Price; and y = the total quantity of all goods and services sold during the time period in question, which is highest when the labor force is most fully employed. Not to get too much in the weeds, but by printing more money and keeping that wealth concentrated in the hands of a minority, therefore decreasing velocity of exchange while raising the money supply, price naturally has to rise, especially when the nation's labor force isn't "fully employed," which is most of the time.

Some argue that if a laborer wants to make more money then he or she should obtain the skills necessary to command a higher salary, and this is absolutely true; however, if a person working over 40 hours a week is barely getting by and therefore has to work a part-time job to make up the difference, they wouldn't have the time or money to obtain those skills, would they? When a firm is allowed to underpay its labor, the burden of private labor expenses get shifted over to the tax-paying middle class, who are then compelled to make up the difference through social services, which are in effect Government subsidizes – exactly the type of inefficiency Adam Smith warned us about.

Alfred Marshall, another founder of modern-day economics, also believed that the duty of economics was to improve the material conditions of the working class; but unlike Smith's faith in the inherent goodness and mutually beneficial results of "laissez faire" (a completely unregulated market) and the "invisible hand," Marshall concluded that the public welfare would only be secured when social and political forces compelled Industry to play fair (as the Nobel-prize winning economist Joseph E. Stiglitz said in 2012, *"The reason that the invisible hand often seems invisible is that it is often not there."*). Publishing his *Principles of Economics* in 1890, Marshall introduced the idea that supply and demand – defined as utility (the demand for a good or product, depending on how useful that good or product is in the consumer's eyes) and cost of production (what the producer gives up to supply enough goods to meet demand) – are the determinates of price.

The higher the demand, the higher the price, especially when the supply is scarce; not necessarily because costs have increased (although clearly more productions costs more), but merely because, well…because the producer knows that she will get whatever she asks for when a good is in high demand, regardless of how much it cost her to produce it (think of the iPhone and most other in-demand tech products, where price far exceeds the cost of production). If costs are high and demand is low, production ceases altogether. But if costs are high and demand is higher, production will continue unabated. Repeatedly, it's demand that drives the economy. Underpaying labor, however, decimates consumer demand, and without demand, there is no production, there are no jobs, and there can't be any profit, either for the producer or the laborer.

Education & the Economy of Debt

But decreased purchasing power isn't just a problem faced by minimum wage workers; skilled workers are facing the same dilemma. Between the 2000-2001 and the 2010-2011 academic year, the cost of higher education has risen 70% from an average of $10,820 to $18,497 for public and private 2- and 4-year institutions. While a college degree has become cost prohibitive for most Americans, those "lucky" enough to secure student loans to fund their schooling are saddled with stunning debt that has far-reaching effects on our entire economy. On September 10, 2014, CNN Money reported that 40 million Americans now hold at least one outstanding student loan, with the average borrower carrying four student loans apiece at an average balance of $29,000; in 2008, those numbers were less than three loans per student with an average of $23,000. The nationwide student loan debt in the U.S. is now a record $1.2 trillion.

This debt isn't the "personal problem" of a select few, as some Americans would like to think: quite the opposite. As of the writing of this book, while the unemployment rate is currently hovering somewhere between 5.8 – 6.2%, the Government's U-6 report (which *unlike* the U.S. Bureau of Labor Statistics' (BLS) unemployment rate, factors in those workers "marginally attached to the labor force" as well as those "employed part time for economic reasons") estimates that the real unemployment rate is closer to 12.6% as of September 2014. Students are graduating but the jobs aren't there, and graduates that struggle to pay off their loans because of a bad economy can't afford to buy new homes, new cars, get married, have children, travel, or purchase extras like dinners out, t-shirts, haircuts, web-site designs, and a slew of other goods and services that small businesses have to offer. If small businesses lack customers, they close up shop. And the cycle continues.

STEM

Realistically speaking, is a non-skilled labor force even an option that any industrialized nation can afford in a globalized, technologically advanced market? We don't just need more jobs, we need *better* jobs, and there's no disputing the fact that America needs to grow its skilled labor force through education; but how do we do this without decimating consumption with high student loan rates? On the one hand, if the U.S. is unable to provide a skilled labor force, Industry will go elsewhere, outsourcing valuable jobs that we need here at home; on the other hand, student loan debt is stalling our economy because it hinders consumerism.

Some people argue, and rightly so, that degrees in "Women's Studies" and "Philosophy of Art" aren't smart choices in a technologically-driven market, and that whomever elects to spend their time and money on an education which teaches skills that aren't in demand is just begging to be in debt; but it cannot be disputed that the U.S. would greatly benefit by a labor pool well-versed in the STEM disciplines (Science, Technology, Engineering, and Mathematics). In 2013, Bill Gates and Mark Zuckerberg partnered up with Code.org, a non-profit organization, to offer computer programming tutorials to high school students in the hopes of sparking interest in our nation's youth for skills that would better serve them, and our national economy – a great example of Industry acting responsibly and realizing that investing in labor benefits us all. But until the U.S. ramps up its education system and catches up to other nations in the STEM fields consistently and across the board (some of these nations being Third World countries, mind you) our economy won't stand a chance in the coming decades. That's not to say that the Arts should be abandoned, because a nation without culture, driven solely by profit margins, is a vacuous and dangerous thing. Just pointing out that the U.S. cannot afford to ignore the market requirements of a technologically driven world.

Tuition Costs vs. Quality of Education

You would think that the United States would have the best education system in the world, considering our prominence on the world stage; and yet, we are lagging behind in comparison to other nations. According to the Organisation for Economic Co-Operation and Development (OECD), the U.S. ranks 26th in education among the 37 industrialized countries evaluated. How is this possible? Are teachers unions the problem, keeping ineffective educators employed even as they fail our students, as some Americans attest? Or are the rising costs in tuition just the result of the astounding increase in the administrative body in our nation's schools? Is quality education being sacrificed in favor of funding bloated administrations instead of on better teachers and the state of the art resources they need in order to educate adequately, such as computers, books, and lectures with subject experts?

It sure looks that way. According to the New England Center for Investigative Reporting and the American Institutes for Research, a nonprofit, nonpartisan organization, "non-academic and professional employees at U.S. colleges and universities has doubled in the past 25 years," doubling the pace of the growth in the number of students enrolling for school, and collectively increasing the number of administrators by 517,636 from 1987 to the 2011-12 school year. That's an average of 87 new administrators added to the system for every working day. Meanwhile, the number of part-time faculty and teaching assistants now make up half of all teaching staff, up one third from 1987.

Many have pointed out another factor: that schools are charging outrageous tuitions because they realize that no matter how expensive tuitions become, the Government is only too happy to offer student loans at ten times the interest rate they charge the Banks; the evidence supports this and of course this practice is indefensible. Why do Americans allow this type of predation against students whose only transgression is a desire to acquire an education in order to get ahead? And how do all of these factors affect the quality and accessibility of education in the U.S.? It's a complicated issue and clearly, this is definitely a conversation worth having.

Start at the Beginning: Primary Schools

A good education starts at home, and it's absolutely true that too many of our nation's children grow up in homes in which they get no academic support, either because their parents are busy working to make ends meet and are largely absent, or because the family dynamic suffers from other dysfunctions, such as drug, alcohol, and domestic abuse. Teachers have long complained that their hands are tied when it comes to educating their students because of parents that won't cooperate with them and administrators that won't support them when parents threaten to sue simply because the teachers are unwilling to put up with unruly and disruptive behavior in the classroom. These factors have a ripple effect that diminish the caliber of our education system across the board; how we deal with these issues is imperative to the health of our economy, as it's all related.

Some claim that the answer to this issue is to build more charter schools, which produce higher test scores and better-educated students; but is building more structures really a solution? Consider what happens when a charter school closes, as many do; the public school system is then responsible for taking those students in and educating them – but without the funds to do so, as they were already paid to the defunct charter school. This puts extra fiscal stress on already deficient educational resources, a no-win situation, especially for our kids. If the success of the charter school system has a lot to do with the greater flexibility they enjoy in their academic programs, why not just reform the schools that we already have and adapt these winning strategies in our public schools, those that so many of our nation's children already depend on for their primary education? If we can't get more kids on track consistently early on, how can we expect them to have the necessary skills to succeed in high school, at the university, and ultimately, in the job market?

Clearly, education and student loan debt are not personal problems, they are very real economic problems that affect the entire nation, and that we'll have to solve together if at all. A vibrant middle class is vital to a stable, healthy economy, and vice versa; if you kill the goose that lays the golden eggs, you can't expect any more eggs…at least, not golden ones. Maybe you can expect invisible ones that you make up with your own imagination – or in the case of the

U.S., that you print out of thin air. But those aren't real eggs, and this is just common sense.

The Rules

Competition breeds excellence and there can be no Free Market without it; in Economics, the term Competitive Markets require a few ground rules, and a market's "freedom" can be judged upon where it lands on the spectrum of competition, which can range anywhere between a highly competitive market where there are many sellers, each of whom enjoys little or no control over the market price of a good; to pure monopoly, in which an entire market or industry is dominated by a single supplier who controls market price (unless subjected to some type of government regulations preventing them from doing so). Notice that regulation is not considered a deterrent to a Competitive Market, as long as the regulation has nothing to do with price setting; in other words, the "freedom" in the market has to do with price setting, not with safety requirements or fair labor laws.

The Six Assumptions of a Competitive Market:

1. There are many suppliers in the market, each too small to affect the price of a good by changing its own supply. For example, if a firm decides to reduce its production, it won't cause the price of the good to skyrocket because there will be other suppliers able and willing to fulfill consumer demand. In this case, each individual firm is said to be a "price taker," meaning, they must accept the price naturally set

for their product by consumer demand. They don't have the power to arbitrarily raise or lower the price of a good across the board in the market.

2. Each firm in an industry produces products that are perfect substitutes for each other, and consumers perceive the products to be identical. Good examples of this are toothpaste, toilet paper, soap, and water. When you have extra cash, you may splurge for a slightly more expensive brand of any of these goods, but when times get tough, you consider the cheap soap/paste/toilet paper/water to be just as useful as the expensive stuff. Few people, if any, would pay, say, $20 for a tube of toothpaste because we all know that a $5 tube would do the same exact job; however, if they have the extra money and want to splurge, they might just commit this lunacy (Ok, ok! It was only once, so sue me!). In the technology industry, some goods will display greater differences in quality, especially when it comes to computers; but in a competitive market, there will be enough computer suppliers providing equal-quality products to meet consumer demand and without any one firm monopolizing the industry.

3. Consumers have perfect information about the prices all sellers in the market charge for a good in order for them to make a rational decision about their purchases. Of course, this doesn't mean that consumers *will* make a rational decision when purchasing a product (see above), but that they have enough information to make that choice if they wanted to. Plenty of consumers will still pay

$5,000 for a suit when they can pay $500, but in a Competitive Market, they will be making that decision based on preference, not ignorance.

4. All firms in the market have equal access to resources such as technology, capital, labor, etc., and any improvements in production technology attained by one firm can benefit every other supplier in the market. This is a strong argument against patents for inventions that are in essence based on inventions that came before them, but which halt any further progress, sometimes for decades. Understandably, no firm wants to invest millions on an invention only to have it profit its competitor who did not buy into its development, but there ought to be some type of legal provision that would prevent firms from monopolizing inventions past the point in which they recoup their initial investment, as well as a reasonable number of profitable years thereafter. Patents that carry on for a disproportionate amount of time only serve to impede the growth that would otherwise benefit us all.

5. There are no barriers to entering or exiting the market, so the market is always open to new competitors. This is a great argument for streamlining regulations and keeping them down to only those that are most necessary for the protection of the consumer, the laborers, and the resources that all firms depend on to function.

6. There are no externalities in production and consumption so there is no difference between

private and social costs and benefits. In other words, all things being equal, good business serves not just the producer but the consumer as well. This is where common-sense controls such as fair labor laws and environmental regulations come into play. No, excessive regulations do not promote a Competitive Market or the needs of the consumer, because they can hinder entry into the market and therefore diminish consumer choice; however, zero regulations has detrimental social effects and eventually work against Industry whose resources and consumer base become decimated through abuse and neglect.

The assumptions behind Competitive Markets weren't constructed willy-nilly; they are the guideposts that ensure Capitalism can function as a system that foments freedom and choice, instead of constricting them. Ignore any one of these requirements and you no longer have freedom-inducing Capitalism; maybe you'll have an Oligarchy (many studies attest that this is exactly the system the U.S. has in place today), and a market place monopolized by the friends of powerful politicians who either turn a blind eye to violations perpetuated by large, multinational corporations, or who write laws to favor their Corporate friends at the expense of other producers, consumers, and laborers. But you won't have Capitalism that facilitates liberty and economic prosperity for all, and you certainly won't have a Free Market. Let's keep these assumptions firmly in mind when invoking the concept of a "Free Market."

Now that we've established a foundation, the following are the seven ground rules that will help us discuss, debate, and deliberate 21st century politics in a way that will increase our chances of effectively defining, promoting, and protecting our rights, freedoms, and interests as a People (say *that* six times fast).

I. Drop your labels.

"The greatest deception men suffer is from their own opinions." – Leonardo da Vinci

Many years ago I was working as a hostess at a famous restaurant in New York City's Meat Packing District, an area of town known for its high-end boutiques, fine eateries, and elite nightclubs; down the street and around the corner I had a friend – let's call him "Steven" – who worked at such a spot. Very exclusive and known only to a select few, the nightclub posed as an inconspicuous, albeit trendy café during the day; but on certain nights the venue became a watering hole for the City's elite partygoers. Of course, being local laborers we were all dying to get in, but who would have us? Bar backs, wait staff, and hostesses didn't really make the cut when it came to Gotham's glitterati, and so we had to devise a plan if we were to get past the velvet rope. Luckily, Steven had an entrepreneurial streak and figured out a way to get us into some of these soirees.

The employees of the café were given black "Staff" t-shirts and black aprons upon employment, but turnover being what it is in NYC's restaurant industry, these t-shirts were no longer useful once an employee quit. Steven was a true philanthropist and hated to see anything go to waste (ahem) and so he graciously offered quitting staff $5 for each of their t-shirts, which they willingly sold to him. Steven would then sell these t-shirts to his friends for $10 a pop, so that we could sneak in on club nights through the employee entrance in the back of the building without detection. Yes there was security manning the front door, but no one was really watching the rear; in addition, coming off our own shifts from a near-by restaurant, we were already dressed in black so the t-shirts looked like part of our uniform. We wore them over our regular tops, and once we got inside, we'd go to the bathroom and peel off the Staff shirts that Steven then placed back in his locker in the basement. We partied plenty of times this way until Steven got a part in the chorus of a Broadway show and quit; when he didn't find work after the show's run ended, he moved back to Oregon to teach yoga. Go figure.

Partisanship vs. Leadership

This story serves to reveal how labels work – if it looks like a duck and quacks like a duck, most people will assume it's a duck, even though it's really just a partier in a duck's t-shirt. Nowhere is this more obvious than in politics. How many times do Americans complain that their favorite candidates, the men and women whose campaigns they volunteered countless hours to, changed positions on the issues almost from the minute they got into office?

This happened to many Tea Party members and Conservatives in South Florida when Senator Marco Rubio ascended into power; having run on a strictly right-wing agenda, Cuban-American Rubio became the darling of the GOP and won the general election in 2010 with 49% of the vote to Democrat Kendrick Meek's 20% and Independent Charlie Crist's 30%. A young, strapping father of four with oodles of political influence under his belt, Rubio went on to the Hill where he promptly spearheaded the "Gang of Eight" immigration reform bill that was nothing short of amnesty – exactly what he claimed to be against during his run for office. On a March 28, 2010 Fox News debate against then-Governor Charlie Crist, Rubio countered Crist's immigration reform platform by asserting that:

> I think that plan is wrong, and the reason I think it's wrong is that if you grant amnesty, as the governor proposes that we do, in any form, whether it's back of the line or so forth, you will destroy any chance we will ever have of having a legal immigration system that works here in America.

Many of his supporters were shocked at how quickly things changed at the Rubio camp.

Now, I'm not saying that Rubio was wrong or right in changing positions – surely he had his reasons – only that his sudden and severe pivot alarmed his most stalwart supporters, the very people who had worked so diligently to get him elected in the first place. This happened because, again, he was wearing the GOP label and the assumption was that he would toe the line and do as he was told; or at least, as he said he would. The subsequent backlash from Tea Party Conservatives compelled Rubio to finesse his once strident, pro-immigrant reform position in a various number of different ways, even going so far as to claim on July 22, 2014, that the bill had stalled due to its lax border-security effort. This is a far cry from his prior statement on June 26, 2013, when he claimed that the bill "mandates the most ambitious border and interior security measures in our nation's history," after Republican Senators Bob Corker and John Hoeven introduced an amendment that toughed up the bill's border security language. Rubio was backpedaling as fast as he could, and it was obvious.

A similar situation was faced by Liberals who had supported President Obama's run for office not just once, but twice; who were left feeling that they'd been severely bamboozled when instead of "Hope & Change," many felt that they were simply given more of the same – an expansion of President George W. Bush's worst policies instead of a complete overhaul and repeal of questionable polity which many felt were threatening our basic civil liberties and rights. Dubya may have signed the disturbing Patriot Act into law, but Obama extended its suspect provisions, expanding the government's domestic spying programs, and creating a 60% surge in the Department of Justice's warrantless electronic surveillance by 2012.

And what of the wars in Iraq and Afghanistan? While Obama did indeed draw down as promised, the tempo and breadth of his drone strike program abroad alarmed most on the Left who questioned both its legality and its magnitude – especially in light of the Court's decision that drone-killing American citizens without due process somehow didn't violate U.S. Constitutional rights. That a Liberal president – one who is a Constitutional lawyer *by trade* – would have come to the conclusion that this strategy was somehow acceptable left many Democratic voters speechless. Some feebly attempted to rationalize Obama's policy, until they realized that they sounded more like war hawks Senator John McCain and Secretary of State Hillary Clinton, than the Progressives they had always prided themselves to be.

Facing the impending retirement of tens of thousands of Baby Boomers, Obama promised to reform entitlement programs such as Social Security and Medicare, two unfathomably costly social programs whose projected payouts far exceed the revenue from which they are supposedly derived; but considering the toxic backlash from Liberal Lefties such as Naked Capitalism's Yves Smith, who accused Obama of wanting to be "the President who rolled back the New Deal," both the Democrats and the Republicans opted to drop reform altogether, preferring to argue incessantly amongst themselves and be accused of "grid-locking" the American political system, than to stick to their guns and face the ire of the American voter.

The Partisan Paradigm

Of course, our elected elite's lack of fortitude won't resolve our entitlement dilemma or our failed immigration laws, but Americans can only blame themselves for it. This type of contradictory pandering is the natural consequence of partisan labels; they not only define your position for you, they curtail your ability to question your party, to criticize other party officials, or to change your mind about policy and what's truly best for the nation. To be clear, there is nothing wrong with a candidate or representative changing their mind, their argument, or their position when facts and circumstances warrant it – but partisan labels and the extremism they inspire in the masses ensure that elected officials can't do it without serious political and social repercussions. Considering the backlash, we can't honestly blame representatives for asking themselves if it's even worth the effort. The more difficult we make it for our elected officials to do the right thing, the easier we make it for them to do the more profitable thing – in secrecy – instead.

Drop your labels.

Both Rubio and Obama went out on a limb and exposed their moderate sides most likely because once in office, they each understood the common sense need to fix a system that isn't working, and may have figured they'd take a more balanced approach in order to solve the issue and expand their base to include Independent, economically-savvy voters; or perhaps they realized that cooperating on their respective agendas would garner them each much-needed support from their peers across the aisle in Congress that they would need to pass pet bills in the future. Whatever the case may be, the results were brutal; and it is precisely the fear of this type of partisan blowback that drives most politicians to make their deals a little bit more discreetly, far away from public scrutiny and any possible negative ramifications. When your constituents' vote is based on emotion, no logical argument will get them to see why a different tactic may be necessary to achieve the same goals. What politician then, would be willing to take a chance on their political career in order to explain to the masses the logic driving a change in policy? Very few, indeed. But again, that's our fault; partisanship is an inflexible, irrational bully that won't take "no" for an answer, and so it drives political activity underground.

The Partisan Ruse

If we peel back the labels however, a totally different political system emerges, one where representatives cooperate more often than not, especially when it comes to advancing the interests of their very powerful friends in the Banking and Corporate sectors. Take TARP, for example. Signed into law on October 3, 2008 by President George W. Bush, the Troubled Asset Relief Program was ostensibly created to address the subprime mortgage crisis that had been designed through the predatory lending practices of the Banking industry. In short, it was a bailout that allowed Banks to get away with economic murder, making bad loans without having to face the repercussions of suspect business practices. It should be noted that these were the same Banks that in 2007 had compensated their top executives nearly $1.6 billion in salaries, cash bonuses, stock options, and benefits including personal use of company jets and chauffeurs, home security, country club memberships, and professional money management. They weren't "struggling" firms worthy of our pity, but behemoth financial powerhouses who made really bad loans and were rewarded for doing so. The American tax payers were on the losing end of TARP twice; not only did they have to pick up the slack to cover the banks' losses, many lost their homes in the banking debacle. The banks, on the other hand, got off scott-free.

TARP money came with no strings attached, basically money for nothing; banks were free to receive it without any obligation as to how it was to be used. The effect was that only a fraction of that money was used to recapitalize bank subsidiaries, and even less was used to increase lending to the private sector; in other words, the Banks received the money but didn't lend it back out, nor did they use it to restock their coffers. The Senate Congressional Oversight Panel, which was created to oversee TARP, concluded on January 9, 2009 that:

> In particular, the Panel sees no evidence that the U.S. Treasury has used TARP funds to support the housing market by avoiding preventable foreclosures. Although half the money has not yet been received by the banks, hundreds of billions of

dollars have been injected into the marketplace with no demonstrable effects on lending.

So, where DID the money go?

The answer is disheartening and infuriating; in 2008, firms that had received a total of $295 billion in TARP money had spent $114 million on lobbying and campaign contributions. While the Obama administration feebly promised to set a $500,000 cap on executive pay at firms that had received the bailout, many insiders considered this promise as nothing more than political posturing, "A joke," according to Graef Crystal, a former compensation consultant at the firm Towers Perrin, and an expert on the subject. According to Crystal, the caps would only allow companies to defer compensation, not get rid of them. "If the government is paid back, you can be sure that the stock will have risen hugely."

But it wasn't just TARP that revealed the nefarious bi-partisanship efforts of our elected officials; it was also the disastrous Patriot Act and its offspring, the NSA's PRISM program; as well as the Stop Online Piracy Act (SOPA) and Protect IP Act (PIPA), two pieces of legislation that would have held Internet Service Providers (ISPs) and social media sites responsible for the content uploaded by their users, systemically imposing the censorship of any sites that were determined as violators, and therefore expanding the powers of your ISP to monitor everything you did on the Internet in order to avoid getting sued for copyright infringement. While giant social media sites such as Facebook and Twitter (both opposed to the bills, by the way) may have been able to pay an army of lawyers and data acquisition specialists to protect themselves from liability, start-ups would have never made it off the ground, as who would fund a venture that could possibly face a bankrupting, frivolous law suit over something which the start-up had absolutely no control?

And what of the impending Trans-Pacific Partnership Agreement (TPP or TPPA)? Started in 2005 under President George W. Bush as the Trans-Pacific Strategic Partnership Agreement (TPSEP or P4), TPP is a secret, regional "trade agreement" amongst the nations of Australia, Brunei Darussalam, Canada, Chile, Japan, Malaysia, Mexico, New Zealand, Peru, Singapore, Vietnam, and the United States, whose policies have been crafted with the "help" of over 600 corporations, and has become one of the primary goals of the Obama administration's trade agenda. Although the pact was set for completion in 2012, the spurious nature of the its title versus its actual methods proposed – especially in reference to contentious issues such as agriculture, intellectual property, and services and investments – has given rise to countless protests worldwide. Amongst its many alarming features, the pact would give Corporations the right to sue participating nations if their State policies negatively affects a firm's profit margin, causing many to argue that TPP would undoubtedly remove all sovereignty from the State and put the territories signed to the pact under the rule of C-Suite Corporate heads and boardrooms.

Alarmingly, this is already happening. In an attempt to alert the illiterate demographic within its population and to further drive home of the dangers of smoking to everyone else, the nations of Australia, Uruguay, and Togo recently switched to graphic warnings on the labels of cigarettes sold in their respective countries. Phillip Morris International responded by suing Australia for "a deprivation of valuable property," suing Uruguay for "substantial privation of property rights," and threatening Togo with an "incalculable amount of international trade litigation." PMI's official response (which can be found on its website, justthefacts. pmi.com) to accusations that it is basically using its power to prevent nations from protecting the health of their citizens, said this:

> Investor State Dispute Settlement (ISDS) provisions in international trade and investment agreements create a fair and transparent process, grounded in established legal principles, for resolving disputes between investors and states. Anti-tobacco organizations accuse PMI of leveraging ISDS provisions to prevent governments from passing tobacco control measures. Specifically, they claim that PMI uses its ISDS cases in Australia and Uruguay as a means to reverse tobacco regulation in those countries. A closer look at the ISDS system and PMI's cases shows that these attacks are unfounded.

But tobacco regulation reversal is *exactly* what happened in Togo, who wasn't actually sued, but was therefore forced to give up its new packaging because it realizes that it's a tiny nation who can ill afford to fight PMI in court. Upon this writing, Uruguay remains undaunted and has instead ramped up its anti-tobacco campaign, stating through Silvina Echarte Acevedo, legal adviser to the Uruguayan ministry of public health, that, "It is our right and duty as a government to protect our citizens' health." However, Uruguay's crusade has cost it dearly in legal fees, and it's been compelled to seek the help of the World Health Organization to cover legal expenses, inspiring former mayor Michael Bloomberg to kick in $500,000 to help Uruguay cover costs. Australia also continues its fight against Big Tobacco, citing the damaging effects of allowing foreign investors to sue governments, which of course is one of the provisions of the TPP. This distinction wasn't lost on Dr. Patricia Ranald, Convener of the Australian Fair Trade and Investment, when Australia's high court ruled against Big Tobacco on the graphic packaging case:

> Some trade agreements have clauses which allow foreign investors to sue governments, on the grounds that a law or policy 'harms' their investment. The Australian government policy is to oppose these clauses in current and future trade negotiations. However, they do exist in some past trade agreements, and big tobacco is taking full advantage of this. The Philip Morris tobacco company is currently suing the Australian government over its tobacco plain packaging legislation, using an obscure 1993 Hong Kong-Australia investment treaty. Philip Morris is actually a US-based company, but could not sue under the US-Australia Free Trade Agreement, because public opposition kept this clause out of the agreement. Philip Morris rearranged its assets to become a Hong Kong investor in order to use an obscure treaty. This shows how giant global companies can abuse such clauses in trade agreements. Big tobacco and other global corporations are lobbying hard to include the right of foreign investors to sue governments in the current negotiations for a Trans-Pacific Partnership Agreement (TPPA) between the US, Australia, New Zealand and six Asia-Pacific countries. We congratulate the government on its victory today and urge it to continue to oppose the

right of foreign investors to sue governments in the
TPPA and all current and future trade negotiations.

How is it possible that a nation's people not be able
to decide and vote on the regulations they would like to
see implemented, without Industry's consent? And yet, our
elected officials are all for another trade agreement that
would allow Industry expanded powers that exceed even
the sovereignty of nations. Proponents of TPP argue that it's
necessary that Corporations have a sense of recourse if they
are expected to invest and innovate; that without the legal
right to sue States for their domestic policies, it's too risky for
private interests to set up shop anywhere. But…isn't risk part
and parcel of Capitalism? Isn't risk an intrinsic characteristic
of *all* business? If risk is removed from the market, then
it is no longer a "free market," it's an Oligarchy – isn't
it? The question then becomes, why would our elected
officials work so diligently to create and pass these blatant
violations of our civil rights and liberties, agreements and
policies that destroy any chance for a "free market," and that
could potentially even threaten our nation's sovereignty?
Easy. Because campaign contributions aren't partisan.
Because campaign contributions trump all. And because
Government consistently rigs the laws in order to benefit
their Corporate sponsors, effectively destroying any real
chance for a "free market," anywhere. Anyone that remains
doubtful that this is the current reality in America is urged
to read Robert Reich's masterful book, "Saving Capitalism."

President Obama will sell the TPP to Congress under
the guise that it will help curb China's power as world
market-setter, and that it would help set "high standards
for protecting workers and preserving our environment." As
good as that may sound on paper, the problem is that these

promises have been made before, but have never actually been realized; President Clinton's NAFTA made these same claims, but never made good on any of them. As skills and productivity failed to meet the standard (read: increased production at ever- cheaper rates), jobs supposedly created to benefit Mexico moved to China, causing displaced farmers to emigrate, most often illegally, to the United States looking for work; only Canadian firms faired slightly better with increased exporting to the U.S., although wages in their country stagnated. And NAFTA did nothing to improve the environment, either: quite the contrary. The only thing that NAFTA was truly able to accomplish in the U.S. was to make the wealthy richer while putting downward pressure on collective bargaining, decreasing wages and worker benefits for labor, and putting small businesses at the mercy of the large, multi-national Corporations that were able to take full advantage of NAFTA's outsourcing perks. So why in the world would we believe that *this* time the TPP will get it right, and that the American People will benefit at all from this secretive pact? It sounds like more of the same to me, and if that's so, then I suppose there really will be no end to cheap labor and Americans will be competing for jobs against the third world. Hello, $2 an hour jobs. Goodbye, American middle class.

FULL DISCLOSURE: Bloomberg Philanthropies and the Bill & Melinda Gates Foundation have partnered up in 2015 and created a fund to help low and middle income nations fight Big Tobacco in the courts, yet another example of Industrial Giants acting responsibly and giving back to the world from which they've made their wealth.

By abandoning partisan labels voters are better able to assess what is really going on with their elected officials. Why should we continue to make excuses for their poor performance and their damaging policies that work against our own best interests? Because they're a member of "our" party? That excuse doesn't past muster. By the same token, why should we continue criticizing and voting against good policies, policies that make sense and that are actually beneficial to our nation, simply because they were fashioned by an official from the "enemy camp"? If a policy is sound, it should be championed and developed no matter where it came from. Standing in the way of good law because of partisanship is, in fact, putting a political party over the welfare of the country; there's nothing patriotic or responsible about that.

Elected officials are there to work for *us,* not the other way around. It is not our job to protect them or to keep them in power when they have shown themselves to be ineffective and duplicitous. We need to stop entrusting our own sense of self to politicians who are complete strangers to us; we are not them. Their failure is not our failure – not unless we keep them in office. So let's not. Let's take a minute to reject the fear of being ridiculed or worse, ostracized, by our "political peers" in order to look at the numbers, do the math, and connect the dots. Like the worst of all used-car salesmen, both Democrats and Republicans are counting on the American voters' unwillingness to look under the hood before making their purchase at the voting booth. Let's stop flinging labels around in a debate, because labels don't clarify, they obscure; and they only serve to cover up the inadequacies of those men and women we pay to represent us. Let's hold their feet to the fire individually by debating their actions and policies, regardless of what party they claim to belong to. Let's get behind the good guys, whoever and wherever they are. Let's stop making insipid, blanket statements like, "All Republicans/Democrats are (fill in the blank)," because clearly, not everyone who wears an [R] or a [D] after their name acts the same way, nor votes the same way. Let's stop giving them a pass based on an arbitrary label.

The truth of the matter is that if the American people want a better government they're going to have to prove it, and the only way to do that is to stop toeing the line for the illusion of a "two party system" that is keeping the nation locked in a no-win situation. And please People, stop feeding the political pundits – a mixed bag of media "experts" and fire starters who make their money from fear mongering and from keeping the country in a constant state of contention. They're not working for you, but against you, all the way to the bank. You're smarter than that. Drop your labels.

II. Ask questions (and listen to the answers).

"Courage is what it takes to stand up and speak; courage is also what it takes to sit down and listen." ~ Winston Churchill

Due to his ability to debate practically any subject no matter how abstract, with virtually any one no matter how inexperienced, Socrates is regarded as the father of Western Philosophy. Plato's *Republic* reveals Socrates' genius abilities in action, and the one action that is repetitive throughout is his commitment to asking questions. Socrates may have believed that he already had the answers to how the seen (and 'unseen') world worked, but had he simply made his proclamations instead of engaging an audience he would've then had to work backwards and spend the rest of his time counter-arguing every protest made against his theories. Instead, Socrates began by asking questions that enabled him to lead his audience down the same logical path that he himself took to reach his conclusions. In this way his opponents came to the same deductions, but instead of casting a doubtful eye on them they easily accepted these ideas as their own, arrived at through the use of their own logic, and based on their own beliefs.

But Socrates didn't just barrage his opponent with questions – *that* would've been annoying and it wouldn't have gotten him very far; he also listened to their responses, which often exposed their train of thought and therefore, what Socrates' next question should be. In addition, their answers and subsequent questions helped Socrates better define his own positions. So it was the combination of asking questions and listening to the answers that allowed Socrates to become a master debater, and adopting this strategy can help you do the same.

The Purpose of Debate

If we think of debating as a battle to be won instead of as a tool to help us fashion a consensus from where we can start formulating solutions, we'll have a difficult time with this method because it goes against our most natural instincts when we feel threatened – to defend and defeat. So the first step is to realign our definition of what a debate is so that it better suits our needs: not as a war to be waged at all cost, but a way to unite resources with those who share our interests in order to create solutions and affect change in our favor. Keeping this end game in mind will help you keep your cool and your focus during discourse.

The second step is to practice. Practice till it hurts. Try it out on virtual strangers first (yes, like on Facebook) and then "graduate" to real-life debates with those predictable people who love to push your buttons (yes, like your obnoxious second cousin at family functions). From there, you can grow and try it out on "real life" strangers; people you meet at political/social functions. And not just those folks you consider "opponents" – remember, you've abandoned all labels, so you don't necessarily have to agree or disagree with anyone based on political classifications – but even on those who share many of your same political ideologies but with whom you differ on a few key issues. Our political peers tend to repeat mantra and bumper sticker logic because they're looking for validation from the group, and they may be expecting you to toe the line and provide it for them. But if you don't agree with them, then you should say so. It doesn't make your argument any more or less valid; only facts can do that. And you never know, you might be providing them with information that they hadn't considered before. Your factual counterargument and the legitimacy of your opposing viewpoint may be the social "safety net" they need to break away from rhetoric that they secretly may not have ever agreed with, but which they feigned adherence to because they feared being ostracized from the pack.

The more you do it, the more you'll get used to it. When you start to see real results from your new approach – a broader base of powerful connections who are able and willing to share their resources with you; an expansion and deepening of your own understanding of the issues; easier, more fluid, and more pleasant communication with others – it will give you all the reinforcement you'll need to build on. You'll become one of those remarkably calm, cool, and collected debaters that is able to cut through the BS and get to the heart of the matter. You will build an audience; your credibility will grow. You will become known as a person who produces results, not drama; as a person whose opinions have merit because you build them upon reason, data, and facts; because you encourage the input of others in your debates, and you value their perspectives. This reputation will attract other problem-solvers in your community to you and will open doors for you through which you can affect the change that would benefit your city, your state, and maybe even you country. These are real goals to work towards, and they are attainable once you have done the work and laid the foundation necessary. You'll have to get out of your comfort zone first, however; and you'll have to break old habits. But considering the possible outcomes, you can't argue that it's not worth a shot.

Overcoming Miscommunication

Asking the right questions requires that we keep the end goal – consensus and solutions – constantly in mind; however, while asking the right questions might become easier as we get used to researching and understanding the issues from many different perspectives, really listening is still a challenge for many of us. There are many reasons why we don't listen to others; below are the most common reasons, how they apply to political debate, and what you can do to overcome them:

1. **Truth.** We're right, the other person is wrong, end of story. This dualism inspires a preoccupation with proving that our point of view is the only correct one to have. We don't listen to others because there's no point; we've already got the "right" answers. We can counter this by expressing our views but remembering that there is more than one way to skin a cat; this way, we are free to listen to others and understand what they're saying, instead of feeling threatened by new information and rushing to shoot down their point of view before we've even heard them out. After all, they may be able to provide us with valuable information that we didn't have prior.

2. **Blame**. The issue at hand is "all their fault," so anything they say will just be an excuse or a cover-up of some kind. Instead, we can admit that there are many factors that affect an outcome, and that problems can rarely be blamed on any one thing, one person, or one event. Also, we can identify our needs and accept that others have needs as well, realizing that these needs may sometimes conflict. That doesn't mean that anyone is "to blame" as much as that some policies might actually be working for others even if they aren't working for us.

3. **Martyrdom.** You're throwing a pity party for yourself and think that you are being treated "unfairly" and that the other person is just insensitive and selfish; you shut out anything they have to say out of hand. Get off the cross and simply accept that not everyone will agree with your viewpoint, and that's ok. They don't have to. This doesn't discount your viewpoint, so you don't have to feel threatened just because it's being challenged.

4. **Insensitivity**. You're blind to the part you play in creating conflict and how your behavior affects others. You don't listen to others because you conveniently forget that they're people too, with many of the same needs that you have. This is easily countered by putting yourself in the other person's shoes: how would you like to be treated and spoken to? Let the answer be your guide. The Golden Rule applies here, big time.

78

5. **Defensiveness**. You can't deal with criticism; in fact, you're afraid of it. Maybe it's something that happened in childhood, I don't know; but you feel that you have to "defend" yourself and your position all the time, not just express it. You also fight for the last word. Lighten up. Realize that there is no truth behind this thought process; you are not *actually* being attacked, just challenged. And if you are being attacked, you can diffuse it by listening and repeating what it is you hear the other person saying, giving them the chance to clarify. Nine times out of ten people revise their aggressive tactics when they realize that someone actually *is* listening, as most people ultimately just want to be understood.

6. **Fear of being controlled**. You have a problem with authoritative speech and are constantly on guard against being "controlled" or "told what to do," sometimes causing your friends and family to point out that it borders on the irrational. Again, you mistakenly feel that you must "defend" yourself; this is a fallacy. Doing your research and having the concrete data to back up your claims can easily counter this sensitivity. When your opinions are backed up by facts, you can state them plainly without feeling defensive. Facts don't need to be defended; facts defend themselves. That doesn't mean that others will agree with you, but at least you won't feel vulnerable to coercion.

7. **Narcissism**. You feel entitled to better treatment from others – either because of your experiences,

your education, your "expertise" on a subject, etc. – and you get angry, anxious, and frustrated when they do not treat you in a manner that is consistent with your sense of self-worth. You convince yourself that they are ignorant, unreasonable, and simply wrong for their views. Take a minute to assess the possibility that their point of view is actually fulfilling a need, a need you may have overlooked or that you have yet to experience. And check your ego; no matter how accomplished you are, accept that you got there with the cooperation of others. No man is an island, not even you.

8. **Selfishness**. It's all about you, and your needs and point of view trump all; not for any particular reason, just because. There is zero room for anyone else's thoughts, experiences, or perceptions. You already know what you want to see happen, and whatever data or information they bring to the table won't stop you from steamrolling right over them until you get your way (whatever that is). You can counter this by realizing that you're being emotional and illogical; first, seek to understand the opposing viewpoint so that you can have a better perspective about what's actually going on. The world doesn't revolve around you, and neither does the nation. You are part of something bigger – a community, a society, and a country – and your efforts should contribute to the welfare of all, not neglect the needs of those who depend on you.

9. **Mistrust**. You harbor a fundamental belief that other people have hidden agendas and only seek

to manipulate you if you take the time to listen to them. Not so. If you've done your homework, you will know the facts and figures well enough to identify a faulty position when you hear one; trust in your ability to calmly point them out and counter them with data if you should encounter them. However, remember also that you don't have to become unraveled and offensive to point out someone's error; if you are secure in your research, you can state it plainly and move on from there. Anyone can make a mistake, including you; by giving others the opportunity to change their position without losing face, you also allow yourself the wiggle room to do the same. This will help ease more open and honest communication, for everyone.

10. **A "fixer-upper" complex**. You feel the need to come up with all the right answers, ASAP. You "listen" only as much as you need to in order to present your ready-made answers to the problems. Your answers may indeed be exactly correct; however, it is easier to help people come to a conclusion when they feel they've reached it on their own. A good way to do this is to ASK QUESTIONS. Socrates was the master of this and it helped clarify his arguments both for himself as well as for those he debated. By asking the right questions, you can gain new perspective, and so can the person answering.

Actively listening will also help you avoid wasting your time. There's no point in carrying on a debate with someone who clearly doesn't share your goal – to understand and to solve problems – but you'll only know if this is the case when you are truly listening to what the other person is saying. Are they being highly emotional? Are they using expletives, stereotypes, and personal attacks instead of offering valid counter-arguments based on facts and mutual respect? If so, you can always excuse yourself, and walk away. And you should.

Expletives and personal attacks are a sure sign that a person has lost control of their emotions and that they've stopped listening. It often happens when a person feels threatened, maybe not physically, but definitely psychologically; when a person's views are being challenged and they don't have any logical way of defending them. Of course, they don't have to defend anything; they're free to change their minds like we all are. Unfortunately however, not everyone understands that this is a choice. When they realize that their opinions were made in error, some people freak out. Others simply change their opinions to reflect new information. This option is always available to you, and it's always the best one to take. Ask anyone.

III. Share the facts.

"In God we trust; all others, bring data." - W. Edwards Deming

"When dealing with people, remember you are not dealing with creatures of logic, but creatures of emotion." - Dale Carnegie

When we were kids, my younger sister and I would drive my poor mother up the wall with our constant bickering, especially as my sister got older and wouldn't stand for me bossing her around anymore (dammit). Our arguments got most intense on the backseat of our Lincoln Town Car because a) we were bored and b) we couldn't physically get away from each other. So we'd initiate fights for fun. (Ok, *I'D* initiate fights, but why split hairs?)

Our mother, being the wonderful person she is, would patiently try to deal with us by explaining things to us in a calm and logical manner; no, we can't stop at Toys R Us today because we have errands to run and toys aren't priorities; yes, we'll get McDonald's but not right now, you kids just ate; if you girls just sit on your respective sides of the backseat there is more than enough space for each of you; etc. However, because the true driver behind our fights wasn't Toys R Us, or McDonald's, or even that we actually lacked space – but simply that *we wanted to argue* – no amount of reasoning would stop our brawling and our repetitive queries of "But why? But WHY? BUT WHY?!?" Finally at her wit's end, our mother would be forced to pull her one trump card in an attempt to end the madness – "Because I'm your mother and I said so – THAT'S WHY!"

Now, clearly "'Cause I said so," isn't a logical argument, but when you're dealing with illogical people, it's sometimes tempting to resort to their tactics. And although it would quiet my sister and I down temporarily, it never resolved the issue motivating our arguments to begin with – that we both wanted our mother's attention and we were willing to accept even negative attention if it meant that one of us could prove to the other that we had gotten it, that we had "won." Although irrational outbursts didn't work to address the conflict between us kids, neither did using facts alone (my sister and I *still* compete for our mother's attention); nor are facts alone enough when debating politics today. If we're going to get through to others when discussing the issues, we're going to have to temper facts with an understanding of the emotions that are driving the contention to begin with (Yes, I just ended with a preposition. Sue me). Because the biggest, most indisputable fact of all is that people don't make decisions strictly based on data, but also, on how they *feel*.

The Science of Debate

In 2006, cognitive neuroscientist and neuroeconomist Benedetto De Martino of the University College London, conducted an experiment that revealed which parts of the brain are employed when we make decisions; specifically, how the manner in which a challenge is "framed" affects our response to it. In his study, 20 men and women were asked to undergo 17-minute brain scans while deciding whether or not to gamble about $95 worth of English pounds. When they were told that they'd get to keep 40% of the money they didn't gamble, the volunteers only chose to gamble 43% of the time; when they were told that they could lose 60% of the money they didn't gamble, they chose gambling 62% of the time. The odds of winning and losing were identical in both scenarios, and this was carefully explained to them at the start; however, the way in which the question was framed significantly altered their decisions. During each 2-second gambling decision, brain scans showed that the amygdala, the part of the brain that processes strong negative emotions such as fear, fired up vibrantly in response. In cases where the test subjects' logic attempted to resist the framing effect, the neural region connected to positive emotions, such as empathy, became activated. In both instances, however, the driving force was emotion, not the math grounding the experiment. Even the participants who were aware of their inconsistent decision-making claimed that they just "couldn't help" themselves.

That's because the brain retains the emotional memories of our past decisions, and by and large it is these memories that motivate our choices in life. In fact, studies have shown that people who suffer a loss of emotion after a brain injury also have difficulty making decisions, as do those whose emotions have been muted due to medication or depression. Economists have long known the power that emotions have over our decision-making, as have lawyers (Ever seen a divorce play out, where each side is willing to incur huge financial losses just to "win" the case? Yikes!), sales people, religions, and of course, politicians and their political parties. By tapping into our vast emotional resources and framing the issues either positively or negatively, political parties are able to skew our decisions at the voting booth and keep us locked in a constant battle with each other in which the only losers are the People. *"What makes you and me 'rational' is not suppressing our emotions, but tempering them in a positive way,"* says De Martino. And this is the secret to constructive discourse.

Much like my sister and me way back when, too many Americans today are rehashing tired, redundant, and inane partisan insults and calling them "debates"; they're not. Real political debate is a tool used to clarify current issues in order to reach a consensus, and because of this, debate requires more than just opinions – it requires facts, data, and most of all, mutual respect. The end goal of any debate is to find solutions; if this is not your end goal, then you are not debating. You are most likely instigating an argument because it feels good to prove that you can get attention and that you can "win," just like I did when I was a kid. Problem is, you're *not* a kid, and so this strategy will most likely blow up in your face.

If this is your tactic, you'll realize that you're not really debating when you come face to face with a *real* debater, someone who can calmly state their argument and back it up with facts and figures in a way that doesn't offend but attracts support. Even more annoying, they're actually willing to listen to what you have to say, credit your strong points, and respectfully explain where you're going wrong in a manner that is so comforting, so understanding, and so "matter of fact," that you'll find yourself agreeing with them in spite of yourself. And that's ok. The reason they're so successful in debate isn't because they're pulling some Jedi mind-trick on you but because they've done their homework and understand the facts; and also, because they understand that you are a human being and that the only way you'll be open to new ideas is if you feel you are being understood, first.

Keeping an Open Mind

The best strategy is to begin by forming your *own* opinions based on the facts (not emotions, not prejudice), then following them up with an appreciation of where your opponents are coming from (another preposition). Of course this will require that you know what the facts *are,* and also, that you're open to different perspectives and understand the validity of the counter-arguments to your position. Sometimes you'll be presented with new information during a debate that you hadn't thought of before; sometimes, you'll be presented with new information that outright discounts your argument. When this happens, you should say so – quickly and emphatically. "That's interesting, I didn't know that. I'm going to have to research that a bit," isn't a phrase that is going to kill you once uttered, and it sounds way better than continuously defending an argument that has already been proven wrong. If you take the time to research the issues beforehand, to stay open to the facts and truly understand what's going on from all perspectives before you attempt to make a claim, it'll save you a lot of time in the end and will spare you from having to backtrack your position if you fail to do so (Ha! "So" sounds like a preposition, but it's not! So there!).

Baggage

Another thing you'll have to do in order to debate effectively is to identify and abandon any emotional ties you may have formed with old opinions that are no longer useful to you. This is way harder to do than research, because so many of your opinions were formed for you by your family, your peers, your religious institutions, and your Government; and they've been drummed into you repetitively since birth. Sometimes it's painful to question our beliefs only to find out that they're wrong; sometimes questioning our own identity leaves us in the uncomfortable position of having to redefine who we are instead of just accepting who everyone else says we should be. While this is a great opportunity for growth, it isn't easy, so keep this in mind when discussing politics with others that have also been misled or misinformed: you were just like them not very long ago, remember? A little empathy goes a long way, and it's imperative if we're going to overcome the problems that we face together as a nation.

The Fear Factor

There are many forces and special interests that depend on you implicitly accepting what you've been told, and they will fight – aggressively – against any attempt to challenge these carefully crafted belief systems. Most make large sums of money off of your acceptance of the status quo, and those who do so are usually involved in the Government and Corporate sectors. They have all sorts of tactics they like to use to ward off inquiring minds, and top amongst these is fear. Fear is a very powerful emotion and a formidable motivator; in fact, it is *the* most powerful motivator according to psychologists. How else do you think that the Patriot Act could have passed muster, if it hadn't been for the terror that gripped the American people after the 9/11 attacks? How else do you think ISIS gained in popularity amongst Muslims in the Middle East, although its tactics are appalling and a lethal threat to all Muslims in the region? Because when people are afraid, when they are in a panic, they are a lot less likely to do the math or to ask too many questions. They are less likely to see the chinks in the armor, or to consider the consequences of what they are being told to do. They are more willing to accept authority and follow directions.

The Government's use of fear to get things done is well documented; in fact, historians will argue that all governments, no matter how benevolent, are founded out of fear. For the sake of argument, let's take the U.S. as an example, although we are by no means the only nation that has employed these tactics. Firstly, it was the fear and intimidation of religious persecution that brought the colonists here to begin with, and also, it was fear and intimidation which later conquered the land from the natives; then it was the fear of living beneath the rule of monarchy and the Bank of England's complete economic control over the colonies that motivated the Founding Fathers to split from England. It was the South's fear of economic collapse versus the North's fear of the destruction of our expanding republic that led to the American Civil War, and the fear of a breakdown of the family unit that inspired Americans to favor the passing of the abysmal 18th Amendment which ushered in Prohibition and which, although it greased many palms in Government and elsewhere, ultimately created the perfect conditions for an unprecedented era of internal violence and organized crime in the U.S. The fear of industrial tyranny and monopolized markets inspired President Teddy Roosevelt to create his "Square Deal" policy to reign in and break down Corporate power, and later, the fear of domestic unrest inspired his cousin FDR to create "The New Deal" policies in order to address the needs of Americans most affected by the Stock Market Crash of 1929.

The fear of Hitler's fascist control over Europe wasn't scary enough to inspire U.S. involvement in WWII, until the attack on Pearl Harbor gripped Americans with the fear that we could, indeed, be attacked on our own soil if we didn't do something to stop it. Likewise, the 9/11 attacks and the fear of terrorism that ensued allowed for bipartisan support of the wars in Afghanistan and Iraq, which produced $39.5 billion for Houston-based energy-focused engineering and construction firm KBR, Inc., a spin-off of oilfield services provider Halliburton Co. (of which, conveniently, then Vice President Dick Cheney had been the chairman and CEO from 1995 to 2000); and a combined $13.5 billion for Agility Logistics of Kuwait and the state-owned Kuwait Petroleum Corp. However, these wars will end up costing American taxpayers over $6 trillion, with absolutely nothing to show for our expense. The fear of terrorism also allowed President George "Dubya" Bush to pass The Patriot Act practically unchallenged, although many members of Congress – from all sides of the aisle – had serious reservations about the constitutionality of the unregulated, ominous expansion of government power over the private lives of American citizens. No matter. President Obama went ahead and reinstated the most troubling aspects of the Patriot Act, and added his own nightmarish clause; the Government now having the right to drone-strike American citizens dead without due process. Because, you know…terrorism. Terrorism is the real enemy, not the destruction of our civil rights and liberties. Besides, you wouldn't mind having them destroyed unless you had something to hide...am I right?

At least that's what you're told as you are bombarded by reports on the imminent threat of ISIS or Ebola or Measles or North Korea or Russia or anti-biotic-resistant bacteria and viruses or...or whatever new horror is being touted in the media to convince you to give them up, voluntarily and without protest. Go ahead and try to have an intelligent conversation about our eroding civil rights with anyone who has bought into the narrative of fear; you will most likely hear a barrage of expletives followed closely by accusations that you are a "communist," a "socialist," a "tin-foil-hat-wearing-Paul-bot" or just a plain, run-of-the-mill "hippie." Funny how some of the most patriotic patriots amongst us are the first ones to forget the principles that our nation was founded on – individual liberty, whether you agree with someone's personal choices or not; our right to privacy; and our right to freely express ourselves. We are still *one nation,* not just a random collection of sundry individuals. We're a team, and as a team we're all affected by the repercussions of policy. But this amnesia is also a result of fear, namely, the fear that sticking to the facts will get us ostracized by our peers. This fear is a very real phobia and can have disastrous results.

Peer Pressure

Toeing the line for any ideology requires that we give up our own thoughts for those that are established by the creators of said dogma and accepted by its followers. What the establishment gets is much needed validation, loyal adherents to buy into their rhetoric, and foot soldiers to advance their agenda. What devotees get in return for their loyalty is social acceptance, the safety of numbers, and a sense of belonging to something bigger than themselves. If any of this reminds you of high school, then you're on the right track. Thinking for yourself is a lonely place because you're bound to piss somebody off, but the reward is just as great; thinking for yourself allows you to judge every situation separately and to suss out the truth from the BS. Because you're not committed defending ideological "absolutes," because you're willing to honestly examine a situation in order to understand it, thinking for yourself exposes the origins of a conflict and reveals its solution. It gives you the power to create sustainable, productive steps towards resolution, justifies those resolutions with facts and numbers, and presents those resolutions in an emotionally empathetic and rational way.

Net Neutrality

A very popular misconception and an effective fear tactic used by politicians today has to do with the current hot-button topic of Net Neutrality. Net Neutrality is the concept that the Internet should be equally accessible to all, where all data is treated equally, providing an even playing field in which to sell your wares, voice your criticisms, learn and research, or whatever else you want to do. Whether you're a huge Corporation or a small start up firm, an established political pundit or a free-lancing blogger, a Net Neutral Internet allows everyone equal access to benefit from the Internet's broad reach and scope. And that sounds just about right to most freedom-loving Americans who realize that technological innovation and free speech have both been greatly augmented since the Internet became an integral part of our world. The Internet today touches every aspect of our society – communication, education, commerce – even our political system. It works for us because it is *accessible* to us, regardless of our economic status.

However, something else is going on with the Internet that is causing broadband providers to attempt to expand their control over its access: the Internet has become cable's greatest competitor in the movie and TV business. Take Netflix. Video now makes up a whopping 70% of all Internet-distributed data, and 50% of that is coming from Netflix alone. Apple TV, Roku, Amazon Fire, Chromecast, even PlayStation 4 are all amongst a slew of products that provide access to movies and television shows through providers such as Netflix, Hulu, and Amazon Prime, without any need for expensive cable subscriptions. Considering that the only thing that kept Cable TV alive for so long was HBO, it's no wonder that broadband providers panicked when the popularity of non-cable programming, such as Netflix's hit show House of Cards, offered consumers quality entertainment without expensive cable subscriptions. Eventually even Time Warner had to adapt in order to avoid imploding; as of April 7, 2015, HBO can now be accessed sans-cable through their HBO NOW service. But broadband providers haven't completely given up looking to cash in on the innovative business models of Netflix and company by attempting to charge them more to stream their content, claiming that their video output is unfairly "slowing down" the Internet connections of those subscribers who aren't watching streaming videos (Uh...but who isn't watching streaming video?). And where's the proof of this "slowing" effect? Cable providers have yet to provide it.

Not only will charging streaming video providers more raise the price of on-demand Internet streaming media, it will lower the number of subscribers and also the number of advertising revenue these providers will gain. The end result will be less consumer choice, less relevant marketing, and more restricted access to pop culture; unless, of course, you can afford to pay the higher fees. Further diminishing options will be Comcast's acquisition of Time Warner Cable, which will combine the two largest cable operators in the U.S., essentially monopolizing the entire broadband Industry from New York to L.A. Instead of simply revamping their own business model, broadband providers are attempting to stifle the competition they face from Netflix et al., by cutting into their profits; but of course, charging more for Internet access will have repercussions far afield of just a video war.

By making the Internet more expensive, by charging different prices for different "tiers" of speed, broadband providers will be restricting fair access to the Internet; what will a restricted Internet mean to small online businesses? What will it mean to students that take online classes, or that depend on Internet access to conduct research and acquire study aids? What will it mean for the quality and variety of public opinion available on the Internet? Sure, huge online publications may be able to pay more for high-speed access, but when most media companies are controlled by larger parent corporations, what does that say about the credibility of their reports, especially when dissenting voices are priced out? What of independent bloggers that provide off-grid perspectives and first-hand accounts of events, just as vital to our collective knowledge as the bigger, more established news portals? Think about it; during the Arab Spring, how many first-hand accounts was the world able to access because of an open Internet? Would we have had the same access to breaking news and eyewitness accounts if those sharing their content didn't have access to the Internet because of they couldn't afford it?

As alarming as these cost-prohibitive tactics may seem (and ARE), Senator Ted Cruz of Texas was vigorously promoting them to "freedom-loving" Americans, even as it restricts their very freedom; which is really confusing. Why would any proponent of the free market advocate for a broadband provider's attempt to monopolize and limit Internet access? Why would anyone buy into the absurd rhetoric that prohibiting Industry's attempt to restrict access to the Internet is akin to a Socialist Government tactic? Because they have been warned to fear Government by the very same elected officials who *work in* the Government. Do you see the contradiction here? Because it's pretty obvious. Ask yourself: what does it mean when an officer of the Government is telling you *not* to trust the Government…? To put it in perspective: if your doctor told you not to trust medicine, what would that tell you about your doctor…?

On February 26, 2015, the FCC ruled in favor of Net Neutrality, identifying the Internet as a public utility and creating policy that according to FCC Chairman Tom Wheeler, will ensure, "..that no one — whether government or corporate — should control free open access to the Internet." This was a major win for the interests of the People over the greed of unchecked Industry. Those in Government who oppose Net Neutrality claim that it seeks to rectify a problem that doesn't exist, and they're right: there hadn't been any threat to a free and open Internet – until now, when broadband providers sought to monopolize a market unregulated. Net Neutrality stops this type of Corporate predation in its tracks.

The People have long been warned to fear any regulation on the market, even if those regulations are put in place to break up the monopolies that kill competition and destroy the free market. Corporations are adept at influencing Government and also using fear to benefit their agendas, and every Corporation's agenda is profit; that's the bottom line. Not "freedom," not "free markets," not "safety," just profit. Americans are under the assumption that Corporations seek to maintain a free market; they do not. Most large Corporations with the resources to control markets would like nothing more than to establish a system that would allow them to do it, and most Government representatives that have been bought and paid for by Industry would like nothing more than to help them establish that system.

Facts are the Best Disinfectant

Sticking to the facts shatters fear because it exposes the unknown and reduces it to manageable figures; this is also why your sticking to the facts strikes fear in the heart of those who are counting on you to follow your emotion over your logic, not in conjunction *with* it. Because sticking to the facts means following the money. Once you realize who is profiting from any situation, the dilemma becomes clear. Yes it's disheartening to find out that your heroes are actually just people looking out for their own best interests, but maybe idolizing elected officials and corporate heads isn't such a great idea after all. Doing so obscures solutions, and again, solutions are the point of debate. To be fair, some policies are born out of good intentions, out of a sense of duty and of solving the issues; but intentions and consequences are two different things. By seeking to understand one another we can get a better perspective on the situation and where policies are failing or succeeding; we can get to a workable consensus, quicker. By sticking to the facts, we can assess whether or not a policy needs to be reformed, or even abandoned altogether and replaced with something better.

The Facts

The fact is that Americans have the right to bear arms and that violent crime is reduced where more law-abiding citizens carry weapons; it is also a fact that people with mental and psychological disabilities pose a real threat to society when they are armed. The fact is that due to a slow economy and underemployment, many working people *do* need public assistance; it is also a fact that subsidizing behavior reinforces it, and if you are subsidizing single motherhood, negligent fatherhood, and irresponsible banking and corporate practices, you will get more of them, not less. The fact is that Social Security funds have long been used as a slush fund, and the results are bankrupting our nation; entitlements in this country need to be reconsidered and reformed. The fact is that corporate welfare is destructive, and that in a free market, taxpayers are not responsible for propping up private interests. The fact is that if a firm is "Too big to fail," it is too big, *period*; and it should be broken down like any other monopoly. The fact is that a free market requires competition, and monopolies are in direct conflict with freedom-inducing Capitalism. The fact is that Americans have the freedom to practice any religion they wish; it is also a fact that your rights end where mine begin, and beliefs do not trump rights. The fact is that although new life begins at conception, the fetus does not have a Constitutional right to its mother's body without her consent; a woman retains the Constitutional right over her own body whether she is pregnant or not. It is also a fact that past a certain point of development, a fetus becomes viable, and three months is enough time for most women to decide whether or not to carry a pregnancy to term.

The fact is that Corporations are *not* people, nor are Corporations recognized as such in the Constitution; Corporations are neither afforded "inalienable rights," nor the civil rights and liberties granted to American citizens. The fact is that a low minimum wage only ensures that taxpayers subsidize the labor of private firms through the welfare system. The fact is that when you de-incentivize work through low wages, you will foment a populace that will demand Socialism instead. The fact is that someone working 40+ hours a week for minimum wage does not have the time or the money to acquire the education that would improve their skills and increase their value in the marketplace. The fact is that educating our labor pool is something that would benefit the nation as a whole, and that without an educated, skilled work-force, we will lose our competitive edge on the world market.

The fact is that Corporate money in our political system is destroying our Republic, and our Founding Fathers warned us of this time and again. The fact is that neither the Government nor the Corporate sectors are fighting for your rights or the rights of any American citizen; they are each on *their own* respective sides, and only support our interests when they coalesce with theirs. This statement in no way vilifies the Government nor the Corporate sectors; it is not a judgment call, it is simply a statement of fact. Fighting for our interests is *our* job. We have the tools to do it – consumerism and public opinion – so stop assuming that either the Government or the Corporations will do it for us.

However, we will never ensure the protection of our rights and interests as long as we're attacking one another instead of challenging the forces that threaten them. Yes, the willful ignorance of a partisan populace *is* very powerful, but it is a power that is being used *against* you, not *for* you. Stick to the facts, but avoid "fact raging" – yes, you might feel some type of stress relief from aggressively unloading a torrent of statistics against your opponent, but don't pat yourself on the back too hard; it's counterproductive and does nothing to foster cooperation amongst the very People you're going to need most to help you create solutions and affect change.

Seek first to understand where your opponent is coming from; take a minute to consider their perspective and why they might have come to their conclusions. They might just have a point. Then, *share* the facts you've learned. Question everything, together. Follow the money. Stop buying into the propaganda coming from those with a vested interest in your unwillingness to do the math. Realize that you are a member of the People, and quit cheerleading for the other two teams; they're not your friends. They are merely "co-habitants," albeit necessary to our way of life. When it comes to politics, abandon any allegiance other than that to the Constitution and your fellow American People.

Obviously, you will come across people who are not interested in debating facts, but in simply arguing; they will try everything they can to push your buttons and get you to react emotionally so that you'll join them in their mindless slugfest. Don't do it. Kenny Rogers once wisely said, "You've got to know when to hold 'em; Know when to fold 'em; Know when to walk away; And know when to run." He must've been singing about these folks. Empathically stick to the facts and leave the religious, racial, gender, generational, and cultural biases to those who must use them for lack of data to validate their claims. Facts are weapons to be used against those who would oppose your interests, not those who share them. Don't hurl facts *at* your fellow Americans; share them, instead.

IV. Play fair.

"Sports do not build character. They reveal it."- Heywood Hale Brown

Nothing destroys the hope for productive debate quicker than a debater who wastes everyone's time by using fallacy in his or her arguments. It adds another layer of muck and mire to get through and discount, instead of just focusing on the issues at hand, which are challenging enough. It's really tempting to use fallacies in debate because, let's face it – they work. Most people aren't fully aware of all of the facts and so they can be easily swayed by a good fallacious argument. It riles them up. And it can even sound like it *might* make sense, at least until after the debate has been "won" and people do some research and realize that the argument doesn't hold water. That's the problem with using fallacious arguments; if you make this tactic a habit, you will build a reputation for it, and you will ruin your own credibility. You will hinder your own potential to reach your goal, which is crafting solutions and affecting change.

We all fall into these traps on occasion but it's important to be aware of them before someone else points them out.

Play fair.

Below are ten ways to avoid using illogical methods in a debate:

How to Avoid Fallacies and Keep Your Credibility Intact

1. **Discount the argument, not the person's character.** Even a broken clock is right twice a day. A fact isn't any less true because it comes from the mouth of a sinner, and neither is a lie any *more* true because it comes from the mouth of a saint. Attacking a person's character could work against you in the worst way; not only will you distract from the issue at hand, you'll be opening yourself up to irrelevant criticism, as well. ("Ad hominem")

2. **Don't exaggerate your opponent's argument just to make it easier to discredit**. And don't misrepresent their argument by putting words in their mouth; stick to what they actually said, instead of adding extra words on your own. [A word to the wise here: If you're hearing voices, this probably isn't the best time to validate them.] ("Straw Man Fallacy")

3. **Don't assume that your premise is true – prove it.** Merely assuming that the premises supporting your arguments are true isn't good enough; either prove the premises to be true with data or your opponent will be only too happy to point out that you didn't. If you can't prove your premises, don't use them to support your claim. ("Begging the Question")

4. **Prove your own claims.** Your opponent is not responsible for disproving your argument. If you make a claim, it's your responsibility to prove it. ("Burden of Proof Reversal")

5. **Keep statistics honest.** When you're using numbers in your argument (and you *should* be), remember to consider all relevant factors and not just those that seem to support your point of view (a great book on this subject is Levitt and Dubner's *Freakonomics;* when you get a chance, do read). If you sought to understand an issue from all perspectives before forming your opinion then this isn't a problem for you, but if you failed to get your facts straight beforehand, your argument's going to be shot down pretty quick by new data. ("Hasty Generalization")

6. **Understand the difference between an "event" and a "cause."** Just because an event occurs before another, doesn't mean that the first *caused* the second. For example, if after I snap my fingers I get a visit from the Publisher's Clearing House people (I refuse to believe this won't, eventually, happen to me), it doesn't mean that me snapping my fingers *caused* me to win their "$5,000 a Week for Life Sweepstakes," does it? Or...*does* it? ("Post Hoc/False Cause")

7. **Don't argue that a claim that cannot be proven or disproven, *must* be true or false.** Just because we can't prove that there is life on other planets, doesn't mean that there isn't. Just because we can't disprove it, doesn't mean there is. ("Ad Ignorantiam")

8. **PLEASE do not pigeonhole an argument down to only two possibilities.** There are literally dozens of possibilities; mention them. This shows that you have a broad understanding of the situation, and that you're not trying to manipulate your audience into favoring one outcome over all the others simply by pretending that the others don't exist. ("False Dichotomy")

9. **Don't argue that one thing is related to another without a logical bridge to connect them.** These are called "Non Sequiturs" and are different from Post Hoc in that Post Hoc fallacies have no casual ("this causes that") relation, whereas Non Sequiturs have no logical ("meaningful") relation.

10. **A million Chinamen *can* be wrong.** Just because an opinion is popular doesn't make it true. This is similar to "Ad Hominem" fallacy, but instead of judging the validity of a statement depending on the character of whoever said it, this "Bandwagon Fallacy" assumes that the sheer number of people who agree with the statement is enough to somehow make it a fact. It doesn't.

Debating logically is imperative to sustaining open communication and productive discourse; it's playing fair. It shows you've done the research and that you assume your opponent has as well, which fosters mutual respect. It shows good faith; you aren't trying to "trick" anybody into thinking one way or another, but simply, you've found that certain policies work better than others, and you're willing to share this information with other People in order to proactively do whatever you can to affect change. You understand that there are many factors that create a circumstance so you're open to new ideas and new data from different perspectives; your mind isn't set in stone, it's fluid and dynamic. You're here to find solutions, not to prove a point.

A Great Fallacy in Action: The ACA

The best current example of fallacy in action is the Affordable Care Act (ACA), aka "Obamacare." Similar versions of health care reform predated the ACA; both President Bill Clinton's proposal of "Hillarycare" (which didn't pass into law), and then-Governor of Massachusetts Mitt Romney's successful "Romneycare" (which ended up providing insurance coverage for 98% of residents in his state) were two early prototypes. A quick reminder: although Mitt Romney went on to later criticize the ACA, he was all for Romneycare and the success of individual mandates at the time:

> I'm proud of what we've done. If Massachusetts succeeds in implementing it, then that will be the model for the nation.

Having had a long and winding history before taking on its present form, the ACA was signed into law by President Barack Obama on March 23, 2010, with the ostensible goal of reforming an expensive health care system that kept too many sick Americans uninsured and which then compelled the Government to pick up the slack of their health-care costs through the Medicaid system. By increasing the pool of policy-holders, the law sought to lower rates across the board, making insurance more accessible to those who needed it the most. About 80% of Americans were already insured when the ACA was implemented, of which 55% were covered by their employers, and 31% were insured through Medicare and Medicaid Government programs. But too often, even insured families ended up having to claim bankruptcy when faced with exorbitant medical bills following a sudden illness or surgery that their insurance providers wouldn't cover, because they were determined to be resulting from a "pre-existing" condition.

Does this sound scammy? Of course it does. Did this system need reform? Yes it did, no doubt about it. But the ACA didn't exactly deliver on its "affordable" promise; while lower income families were able to obtain insurance, millions of middle class families that already had insurance saw their premiums increase significantly. And although President Obama had promised Americans, "If you like your health care plan, you'll be able to keep your health care plan," millions of individual policy holders had their plans terminated in the fall of 2013 either because they became too expensive to sustain, or because they didn't meet the new law's insurance standards (the President later publicly apologized for any loss based on his prior assurances).

Americans that never supported Obamacare to begin with are blaming the ACA for an increase of part-time work and decline of full-time employment, although there doesn't seem to be enough data to fully support this claim; however, it should be noted that because firms with less than 50 full time employees would not be penalized for failing to provide insurance coverage to their workers, it's conceivable that many employers looking to avoid penalties and costs altogether began to roll back working hours for their labor before those penalties kicked in. While some firms did end up hiring more employees, seemingly decreasing the unemployment rate, it was primarily for part-time work and therefore has only caused the *under*employment rate to climb. It should be noted that the employee mandate goes into effect in 2016, so at the time of this publication, the true effect of the ACA on employment is yet to be seen. Reform is a complicated matter and reform on this scale even more so; there are still many uncertainties and conflicting data surrounding the ACA, but one thing is for sure – although the ACA was created to address an inadequate health care system in theory, in practice, it ended up backfiring in a myriad of unintended ways. And once again, the middle class got it, right between the eyes.

Real Solutions to the Health Insurance Problem

One of the main reasons the ACA has failed to deliver is because it was built on the fallacy of a *false dichotomy* – that Americans had to choose *either* between the system as it stood, *or*, the ACA as it was written. There are, of course, other choices that would bring down costs and increase the quality of service – for example, the full repeal of the McCarran-Ferguson Act of 1945. Also known as Public Law 15, the Act exempts insurance companies from federal regulation and also allows them to avoid federal anti-trust laws; in other words, insurance companies are allowed to monopolize the insurance markets because the 79th Congress decided that insurance isn't "commerce," and therefore, cannot be regulated under the authority of the Commerce Clause of the U.S. Constitution. Ironically, this was also the decision that allowed Obamacare to pass into law; because insurance isn't "commerce," then it's not unconstitutional to compel citizens to buy it (Does any of this make sense? Isn't "buying something" defined as "trade"? And isn't "trade," commerce *defined*?).

Thanks to the McCarran-Ferguson Act, which also allows states to establish their own mandatory licensing requirements and to regulate insurance companies themselves (making it very tempting for state-level representatives to go easy on their friends and campaign contributors in the health insurance business), health insurance companies are in effect free to collude, fix prices, and set their own markets without repercussion or oversight from the Federal Government. This Act destroys the Free Market competition that would compel firms to lower prices and increase the quality of the services they offer in order to attract more customers. They don't have to worry about attracting more customers; they've already cornered the market. You can take it or leave it.

On February 24, 2010, exactly 27 days before President Obama signed the ACA into law, the House of Representatives passed the Health Insurance Industry Fair Competition Act, voting 406-19 in favor of repealing the antitrust law exemptions granted to insurance companies (notables that voted against the Act were House Minority Leader John Boeher of Ohio, and Rep. Paul Ryan of Wisconsin). The bill was headed by Rep. Thomas Perriello of Virginia and Rep. Betsy Markey of Colorado, and was lauded as a pivotal step towards restoring Free Market principles to the insurance market, putting patients and doctors back in control of health care.

The bill, titled H.R. 743, wasn't introduced to the Senate until February 15, 2013, where it promptly died.

This is what happens when Industry is allowed the unregulated "freedom" to operate as it sees fit. You don't get a utopian world where service to the consumer takes center stage due to some "invisible hand" moved by self-interest. You get collusion for gain. You get less choice. You get price setting. You get stifling monopolies.

This is what happens when Industry is allowed to buy influence in Government. You don't get representatives that bring their constituents' needs to the table. You get representatives beholden to their Corporate campaign donors. You get representatives that promote Corporate profits first. You get representatives that vote against the interests of the People.

Those who argue in favor of allowing insurance to monopolize the market claim that it's necessary in order for companies to share "rate-setting data," but it doesn't take a genius to figure out that this is simply untrue. With today's technology, firms all around the world have access to valuable data-mining stores that they can use to determine the needs, incomes, ages, and all sorts of information about the demographics in whatever market they are operating within; there is ZERO need for insurance companies to monopolize in order to acquire relevant data about their potential customers. That anyone would attempt to advocate for this indefensible vulgarity of a law under the guise of "data sharing" is beyond the pale.

Pretending for a moment that we don't actually live in the 21st century and that this technology isn't actually available to firms, the issue of rate-setting information can still easily be resolved by passing an antitrust exemption repeal that would allow for "data sharing" between firms, as the previous version of H.R. 743 – H.R. 3596 – did. Mysteriously, this allowance was dropped from H.R. 743, without any explanation whatsoever. Real reform was shelved, and instead we wound up with the ACA and all of its uncharted ramifications.

Chargemasters: The Uglier Truth

But while repealing the McCarran-Ferguson Act seems like a great idea – and it is – it still wouldn't get to the bottom of what is truly ailing our healthcare system. The U.S. healthcare industry and the drivers that function within it are like an onion; just when you finally peel back one layer, you realize you've got more than a few left if you want to get to the core of the problem. If you want to get the right answers, you must ask the right questions, and arguing about how the high costs of health care *should* be paid ignores even more pressing, more revealing questions – *why*, exactly, are costs so high to begin with; and *who*, exactly, is setting them? At the core of the failing U.S. healthcare onion, are the hospitals.

On April 4, 2013 Steven Brill wrote a special edition of *Time* magazine, "Bitter Pill: Why Medical Bills Are Killing Us," a scathing piece that exposes the predatory price-fixing by U.S. hospitals as the greatest threat to the American People's ability to access affordable healthcare. The underlying drivers of healthcare costs are varied and inconsistent hospital "chargemasters" – mysterious, inexplicably arbitrary metrics that determine the prices for everything from an aspirin to a CT Scan without any rhyme or reason to justify the expense, nor with any set controls to prevent exploitation; according to one unnamed hospital chief financial officer interviewed by Brill, chargemaster rates "were set in cement a long time ago and just keep going up almost automatically." While Medicare and large insurance companies with the leverage (i.e., the membership numbers) to negotiate these obscene prices might be able to pay less than chargemaster rates, the costs themselves are still hyper-inflated enough to provide more than a hefty profit for the nation's largest "non-profit" hospitals. Of course, People who are neither covered by Medicare nor insurance *are* saddled with outrageous chargemaster rates, and Brill's report is full of numerous accounts of Americans who have either seen themselves go bankrupt because of one-time emergency care or unexpected long-term care bills, or who have seen their savings eaten up slowly and painfully trying to pay them off.

Even more alarming is the fact that insurance providers are currently fighting a losing battle because their bargaining power is diminishing exponentially; large non-profit hospitals are consolidating, buying out rival institutions and private doctors' practices, leaving little option for either the insured or the insurers. This type of monopolization is not only unethical it is profoundly dangerous; when the healthcare of the American People is controlled by an ever smaller group of providers for profit, a group of providers who are neither being regulated nor restrained from the complete take-over of an industry that literally controls life and death, what does that mean for our national security? Obviously this encroachment of private firms into the most vital aspects of our national interests will cause Government to stand up and take notice, to fight these efforts through the enforcement of anti-trust laws, right? Wrong. Touting the benefits of greater efficiency in service (although evidence of efficiency is still left to be seen after decades of consolidation), the courts overwhelmingly ruled in favor of the monopolization of non-profit hospitals that is at the root of our present predicament.

The warning bells were sounded loud and clear during a pro-market, 2013 American Enterprise Institute panel on healthcare, led by prominent economic and legal scholars who warned that hospital mergers over the past 30 years were to blame for the creation of an "oligopoly" with the power to charge prices that far exceed normal market values in a competitive market. Former Medicare administrator Bruce Vladeck described the current system as "a massive environment for the reallocation of income" from households and employers to the private firms that provide care. While the Supreme Court recently ruled in favor of upholding the Federal Trade Commission's power to challenge monopoly-creating hospital deals in the state of Georgia, it might be too little, too late. Carnegie Mellon economist and current Director of the FTC's Bureau of Economics, Martin Gaynor, remained somber. "Once there's been a lot of consolidation it's very hard to undo. Unfortunately a lot of that has already occurred in the hospital sector."

The Affordable Care Act will only exacerbate this problem by creating a new structure known as the "Accountable Care Organization," a collection of providers at different levels of care that will coordinate with each other and oversee the entire course of a patient's treatment. In this way, ACOs will be accountable for every aspect of a patient's healthcare needs. But if these ACOs are allowed to grow as large as non-profit hospitals have been able to, prices are sure to keep rising, while quality of care will devolve – the exact opposite of their intended purpose. The threat of hospital mergers to affordable and efficient healthcare is clear, it seems, to everyone except our lawmakers; *why* isn't Congress stepping up to address this problem? Because hospital and physician representatives have been lobbying Washington for years, asking our elected officials to ease up on existing anti-trust, fraud, and abuse laws that would curb the size and scope of ACO's power. And it seems that Congress, once again, is following orders from their friends in Industry.

Lobbying Health

To put the corruption and influence of the Healthcare Industry on our political system in perspective: defense/aerospace industries and oil/gas interests have spent $1.53 billion and $1.3 billion lobbying Washington since 1998, respectively; the pharmaceutical/health-care-product industries, together with organizations representing doctors, hospitals, nursing homes, health services, and HMOs, have spent $5.36 billion during the same time period – almost double the efforts of both the Military Industrial Complex and Big Oil combined. It's not difficult to see who calls the shots. Unfortunately, the People don't have the kind of money to effectively compete with the interests of Industry, and so key players in Government continue to promote the agendas of Big Medicine over the needs of the People, distracting us from what's going on with contentious partisan arguments about *who* should pay for *what*, so we won't take the time to consider *why* we're paying so much to begin with. And we fall for it, every time.

Unregulated Big Pharma in Action

If you've ever argued against regulating Industry and for keeping health in the hands of those who are driven by profit, take a minute to consider the case of Martin Shkreli, a former hedge fund manager who after acquiring the drug Daraprim through his start-up company, Turing Pharmaceuticals, immediately raised the price from $13.50 to $750 per tablet. Unfortunately, this isn't an isolated case: the drug Cycloserine, used to treat a multi-drug resistant strain of tuberculosis, was acquired by Rodelis Therapeutics and the price sky-rocketed from $500 to $10,800 for 30 pills. The list goes on. And how do our elected officials protect the health of the People against Corporate greed? They don't.

Is this really the Government that we want? And why would any American defend and even champion this predation in the name of "freedom" and a "free market," even as *we* end up footing the bill and lining the pockets of those in power? Fallacies are easy to detect when you know what to look for; stop reacting and take a minute to really listen to what's being said. Commit the list of fallacies to memory so that you're better able to determine when you're being taken for a ride, and also, to keep your own arguments in check lest you fall into this trap. There are so many one-liners and popular quotes out there, repeated ad nauseum by adoring devotees when challenged in a debate, which are built on nothing more than paper-thin fallacies; don't be intimidated by them just because the person being quoted is an "expert" in their field (a few famous economists come to mind). Don't accept any argument as true out of hand; digest what's being said and if it's founded on a lie, a deception, respectfully point it out. Considering the harm that exposed fallacies cause to the reputation of those who use them, and the unsavory taste that they leave in the mouths of those they are used against, avoid using them in a debate.

Nobody likes a con artist; don't be that guy. Play fair.

V. Change your mind.

"Progress is impossible without change, and those who cannot change their minds cannot change anything." – George Bernard Shaw

Think back to when you were a kid. If you grew up in the 80s like me, you were probably roller skating or riding your 10-speed around your neighborhood, or skateboarding. Maybe you were playing with Barbie and her Dream House, or your Bionic Woman doll. Or your Easy-Bake Oven. Or your Star Wars actions figures. You get the idea. My point is that you don't do these things anymore. You grew, and you learned how to do new things. You had new experiences and those experiences changed your perspective and in turn changed your beliefs. If you grew up in America, you probably believed in Santa Clause at some point, maybe even the Tooth Fairy if you had really nice parents. But it would be weird if you still held the same beliefs today that you did back then. The only way that would be possible is if you had never had any new experiences, if you had never grown up.

The opposite of growth is stagnation. Have you ever smelled a stagnate body of water? Holy smokes. That's because anything that stagnates, that doesn't move, that doesn't grow, rots. It rots even as it stands there, a standing body of putrid decay. Nobody likes putrid decay. It's gross. It stinks to high heaven and infects everything around it in the worst possible way.

Unlike reeking bodies of stagnate water, a stagnate mind is a lot harder to detect, even when it's our own. Strike that – *especially* when it's our own. That's probably the hardest of all to detect, because we're too close to it to see it for what it really is. When we stagnate, we don't abandon old ideas and beliefs that have outlasted their usefulness; instead, we coddle them, defend them, justify them, and protect them. We identify our very selves with them. If we're not careful, they become a security blanket – a "woobie" like the one in that classic Michael Keaton 80s film, "Mr. Mom" – a filthy, smelly, yet beloved rag that's never seen the inside of a washing machine. We can grow really, really attached to old ideas and old belief systems, even after they've stopped serving us, because they provide something that seems familiar and safe to us in a world that is always changing and is sometimes frighteningly confusing. Our beliefs become life savers in the ever-changing sea that is living; we can't imagine navigating the ocean of life without them, so much so in fact, that we can miss out on other ways – better ways – of getting along without going under.

Alternatives

For example, we can learn how to swim. We can even get good at swimming and learn to enjoy the changing tides. We can learn how to surf, and ride the waves instead of fearing them. We can inflate a raft or work with others and build a boat; we can throw a net off the side and actually benefit when the sea is most turbulent. We can use sails and motors to route our own journeys, to get ourselves where we'd like to go. Or we can sit it out on deck and get a killer tan. We can do any one of these things depending on what makes the most sense to us at any given time. We have the flexibility to choose. There's no fast rule that says that once we don a life saver, we're stuck with it for the rest of our lives.

Sometimes, however, when we try to take our life saver off, the people around us (who themselves wear a similar life saver), keep it snugly secured to our midsection. Why? Because reevaluating our life savers would force them to reevaluate their life savers as well. And that's a really scary thought for some people, even scarier then the thought of missing out on a nice day on the water. In psychology it's called Cognitive Dissonance, and it refers to the mental stress that some people suffer when they're confronted with new information that conflicts with their preexisting beliefs, with their life savers.

So they use all sorts of tactics to manipulate us and make sure that we don't dare make that change; that we won't even consider it. Here are just a few of them, but I'm sure you can think of others:

The Top Three Manipulation Tactics

1. Intimidation.

Intimidation isn't always overt; in fact, the most effective kind is usually really subliminal. It can be couched in a scathing joke at your expense, or in aggressive criticism of those who don't belong to "the group," of those who think differently, and especially of those who once upon a time *did* belong to the group, but left it, abandoning its tenets. This happens a lot in the military and in the police force, both dangerous careers that require full buy-in from their members in order to function effectively. But it also happens to regular folks in less risky industries. I once knew a young woman who worked in the media and was very politically active, but only along her family's strict party lines, even though she didn't always agree with the rhetoric she was helping to spread. Sounds nuts, right? So why would she do it? Because she was afraid she'd be cut out of her grandmother's will if she didn't. Where'd she get that crazy idea? Her grandmother, of course.

This tactic is what keeps people in gangs, keeps peers from speaking out against bullying in middle school, and keeps fraternities silent when its members are accused of rape and other heinous crimes. The threat could be physical, but it doesn't have to be; it can be economic or social and work every bit as well. This tactic is what helps to keep folks from challenging the "two-party" system and instead, keeps them picking and sticking to a side, either because they're afraid of being ostracized and mocked by their peers, friends, and family within said group; because they're afraid of pissing off powerful, local politicians who could make it difficult for them to acquire a business permit or some other necessary public good; or because they're afraid that they'll be targeted for stepping out of line, possibly losing their jobs, their chances for career advancement, or their business connections as a result. Which is total bull.

If people truly value you and what you have to offer, it shouldn't matter what your political views are. Your political views are only that – views. And all views change depending on where you're standing. If you're living a rich, full life, you will enjoy the view from many different perspectives on your travels as the elevation of your path changes, and as you come into contact with other people who will share their own perspectives with you. Changing your mind is only logical then; anyone who says different is probably trying to sell you a bridge.

Another effective intimidation tactic is something psychologist Anthony R. Pratkanis referred to as "fear-then-relief" in his seminal work, *The Science of Social Influence.* In this scenario, those controlling you are "rescuing" you from a sudden and formidable threat. We've all heard of the old stand-by, the "good cop/bad cop" routine, which is strangely compelling even when you are consciously aware of what's going on. After the good cop "saves" you from the bad cop, you are that much more willing to answer any of his or her questions, you are that much more open to cooperating with them; you are just so relieved that the threat is gone. This tactic can be adjusted to other scenarios as well: the manager who warns that due to budget cuts there will be lay-offs, but probably not your job – then turns around and asks you to work through the weekend; the real estate agent that warns you that there are three other offers on your dream home, but that he's there to help you land the deal, which will be easier for him to do if you just raise your offer; the politician who warns you that the economy will tank and we'll all be standing on food lines by the end of the year, unless, of course, you allow her the ability to turn things around by voting her and her policies into office.

Intimidation and fear tactics are dirty tricks but you can outsmart them if you are able to keep a clear head and realize that being forced to take a stand or "pick a side" while in a state of fear is probably a sign that someone is pulling your strings. Don't let them. Wait until you've had time to think things through before you make any decisions.

2. Guilt

Ah, guilt. It works. It's every mother's secret weapon (I know, I am one) and most personal trainers' tool of choice. If they can't scare you into complying, they can always make you feel like you're killing a kitten if you don't. How many times in our childhoods did we get lambasted with stories of starving children in Africa when we refused to eat our vegetables? How many times do magazine covers and Nike commercials subliminally shame us for not hitting the gym? Even wounded warriors and amputee athletes have gotten in on the act; have you *seen* the pictures of Josh Sundquist and Steph Reid?!? Holy moly. Seriously, what *is* my excuse?

Guilt is the glue that keeps most families and religious institutions intact. Both are famous for creating questionable traditions and beliefs, many of which are passed down unchanged and unchallenged through generations so that they don't always make, shall we say…*sense*. Perhaps they made sense *before*, like when they were first formed, forever ago. But with each new generation the utility of these traditions and beliefs tends to wane. To be clear, there will always be traditions and beliefs that stand the test of time, and rightly so – holidays, for example. They're fun. Or annual family get-togethers. Charity work. Forgiveness. Detachment. But when a belief system formed 1,000 or even 50 years ago doesn't serve a real purpose anymore, when it actually hinders the welfare and progress of its members, then it stands to reason that it's ok to change or abandon it.

However, groups which require a lot of buy-in from their members in order to exist frown upon abandoning or modifying any traditions no matter how nocent, because it's the *willingness* to adhere to these traditions and beliefs that becomes the defining factor of the group, not necessarily whether or not the traditions and beliefs make any sense.

Because they need to know that you will willingly set aside your own thoughts and common sense for the sake of Groupthink. It's the only way for the group to verify that it has total control over you, that it can count on your unflinching loyalty. Think back to the story we all heard as kids, "The Emperor's New Clothes." Sure the guy was walking around naked but no one wanted to say so because it would mean that they would no longer belong to the group. All groups have their own version of selective perception and willful ignorance. All groups turn a blind eye to something they'd rather not admit to, and it's their willingness to ignore the truth that then becomes the prime requirement when granting membership to the collective.

Guilt works even when intimidation doesn't because while intimidation makes someone else the bad guy, guilt makes YOU the bad guy. And most people don't want to be the bad guy. While intimidation threatens you, guilt shames you. It sounds like this:

> Oh, are we not good enough for you anymore now that you've gone to college? Well...maybe you're right. We're not educated people, after all. What do we know? We're just 'regular folk,' working hard just to make ends meet. I don't blame you for not wanting to (fill in the blank) anymore. I'm just glad we could afford to send you to the University; we're all so proud of you, 'College Girl!' (Cue super-dramatic, emotionally devastating background music.)

The underlying message here is, "We've done something for you; you owe us this." It's like throwing your neighbor a surprise birthday party, and then asking him to dog-sit for 2 weeks while you go on a family vacation, a tactic highlighted in Dr. Richard Perloff's book, *The Dynamics of Persuastion*. There's really no way for him to say "no," is there? See? Guilt works.

This tactic also works in politics, where guilt rules supreme:

> You're a Conservative, are you? Why do you want to kill old people and poor kids? Because obviously you don't support welfare for the needy and you want to end Social Security for our seniors. How can you be so heartless? Only a monster wouldn't want to save the lives of children and the elderly. You people make me sick!

Or:

> Oh, you're a Liberal, are you? A baby killer who wants to keep everyone poor and on welfare. How can you support abortion? What about the babies' choice? You only want to expand welfare so that you can lord over the less fortunate and keep them voting for you forever. Not only that, but you also support Government-mandated 'Death Panels.' You people make me sick!

Notice how membership to either group carries the same stigma – that of wanting to kill children and the elderly, and of wanting to keep the poor disenfranchised. Weird, right? Because if Liberals and Conservatives are on "opposite sides," then how can they both have the exact same evil agenda? Where'd we get these strange ideas from, anyways? Regardless, it seems that our seniors, our kids, and the poor are on their own, no matter who is in power. Maybe they should consider starting their own party...?

One thing is for sure; whenever you hear "the children,'" "the elderly," and "the poor" being conjured up simultaneously, you're about to get snowed. They're often used as pawns and emotional triggers to deflect from the facts and turn the argument into a blame-game because they are both the most defenseless members of our society and also the groups with the weakest political voice. Don't fall for it. And certainly, don't indulge. When you're faced with this tactic, simply address it. For example:

"No, I don't want to kill kids and the elderly; well, sometimes I do, but only those in my own family. I mean, who doesn't – *am I right?*"

Regard for the welfare of our most vulnerable citizens is common ground for us all; using them to guilt one another into thinking that our views are somehow malignant is silly. It's hitting below the belt and it's assuming that your opponent is somehow less human than you are. We have to break away from this mentality and realize that we're all in the same boat, together. Our common concerns – our families, the economy, and national security – are part and parcel of our collective foundation; we need to work towards strengthening it, not undermining it by pretending that we somehow don't share these common interests. If we don't learn to cooperate, we'll continue to get fleeced by forces that have learned to pull their resources successfully, to our detriment.

Benjamin Franklin once famously said, "We must all hang together, or assuredly we shall all hang separately." True dat.

3. Flattery

Of these three manipulation tactics, flattery is by far the most powerful. It is so profoundly seductive, so insidious, and so utterly enticing that few people if any are able to defend themselves against it. Unlike intimidation which uses the fear of harm or ostracism to control you, or guilt which turns you into a sinner constantly trying to make amends, flattery pets you on the head and validates what you've secretly, always suspected to be true – that you are special, admired, and relevant. Flattery is the crack of manipulation tactics.

Napoleon Bonaparte conveyed this sentiment perfectly when he said, "A soldier will fight long and hard for a bit of colored ribbon." So true. When my husband was a sergeant in the Army he would constantly come home with ribbons and accolades of all kinds, proudly displaying them but ignoring the reality that I was perhaps too quick to point out – that neither ribbons, nor medals, nor certificates translated into anything of real value, of real worth, for our family. He was making huge sacrifices and was getting a pat on the back in exchange. It didn't seem like a fair deal then, and it doesn't now; but those honors kept him doing a great job without demanding much in return because they validated him on a deeper, emotional level. They "proved" that he was good at what he did, that he was a valuable team player, and that he was admired by his peers and superiors. And that, somehow, was enough.

This also happens often in business. When you want to keep a good employee in your firm but don't necessarily want to increase their pay, all you have to do is "promote" them by changing their title and giving them a trophy at the annual Corporate awards ceremony. It's amazing how many people will settle for greater responsibility without any monetary compensation as long as their title sounds more impressive than it did before their promotion. They sometimes reconcile this disparity by stating that it's gonna "look great on the résumé" and that it's not really a lateral move because they'll be learning new skills and that's valuable in and of itself; but of course, they overlook the fact that they'll be taking on more work and more stress for the same salary, and that their employer will be increasing their own profit margin without incurring greater expense. All of this is lost on them the minute they get that title. It's the emotional equivalent of getting a "gold star" in the third grade for a job well done.

Flattery works in all circumstances, in all groups, with the vast majority of people, and again, this is especially true in politics. We've all received media from politicians and political parties, especially during an election cycle; and how do these letters asking for our time and money start off?

"Dear friends…"

And what do we think? That they don't know us and we don't know them, which is usually a prerequisite of friendship? That they want something from us, and so are maybe being a tad bit disingenuous? NO! We think:

FRIENDS! WE ARE 'FRIENDS' WITH OUR ELECTED OFFICIALS! WE ARE 'FRIENDS' WITH POWERFUL PEOPLE WHO ARE ALSO MEDIA STARS! WE'VE MADE IT!!! WE'VE FINALLY MADE IT!!!

And then we proceed to do whatever it is that they ask us to do, whether it's handing over monetary contributions or countless hours volunteering at their campaign offices, because, you know… we're *friends*. And also, because they occasionally swing by the campaign office and take pictures with us that we can then post up on Facebook and Instagram to prove to our *other* friends and family that we are really going places. So there.

See how that works?

But politicians – who are clearly just trying to make a buck like the rest of us and can't *really* be blamed for trying whatever tactics seem reasonable in order to garner the cooperation of the voting bloc (ahem) – aren't the only political players guilty of this strategy; the other members of our political party of choice will succumb to the same behavior, even though they don't really gain anything as quantifiable as political office. No matter which "team" you play for, there will be plenty of members who will assure you that you are "compassionately working for the welfare of the nation," that you are "right," and that you're a "true patriot" merely through your membership to their particular club. The other side is of course filled with mindless barbarians who are easily misled and who don't understand simple economics or the Constitution, but OUR team, well…we *definitely* know what we're doing. And thank goodness you were smart enough to side with us, because you are truly an asset and we couldn't do it without you.

SEE HOW THAT WORKS?

So what happens when you challenge the status quo, when upon researching the circumstances surrounding the issues, you begin to question the tenets and the rhetoric of your party? You don't. Because the truth is, it feels so darn good to be socially validated, to be part of a group that hands you a pin, a bumper sticker, and a t-shirt, allowing you to walk around with a badge of distinction proving your worth to the world. Proving that you 'belong.' Heady stuff, this flattery.

The Price of Membership

Of course, this does nothing to solve our issues as a People. When we consciously choose to ignore reality in favor of social acceptance, we give up the flexibility and credibility necessary to influence change. That badge of honor we so proudly display is really nothing more than a billboard stating to the world, "I have given in to Groupthink. You've been warned." How is that going to attract the broad support you'll need to create and implement solutions?

Your thoughts are your own and you have the freedom to change them at will; no one has the right to tell you how you are 'supposed' to perceive something. Your thoughts are the one thing that no one can take from you. Changing your mind about an issue doesn't mean that you have abandoned who you "are," because your thoughts don't make up your character; your actions do. And what would this world look like if nothing ever changed? Now *that's* a scary thought.

This also means that others have the right to change their minds, as well; give them the leeway they need to do so. We've all heard debates where inevitably, someone brings up a point that is then attacked, not because it's not valid, but because the person making it has taken a different position from one they used to have:

I thought you were a (fill in the blank), Larry? That's not very (fill in the blank) of you! I guess you've finally realized I was right all along. (Insert smug snicker here.)

This tactic is lame, intellectually lazy, and counterproductive. If you embarrass your opponent for changing their mind, you will only force them to continue to defend ideals that they no longer believe in, ideals that no longer serve you *or* them. Just like you are able to grow and learn and change your mind, so is everyone else. Defend your right to do so by allowing others to do the same. People are much more open to new ideas when they feel safe to change their minds without losing face.

Don't be afraid to question everything. Don't be afraid to grow and learn; it's healthy, it's what life is all about. And especially, don't be afraid to change your mind; it's yours to change as you see fit.

VI. Switch sides.

"Honesty doesn't heal; empathy does." ~ Dan Waldschmidt

It was my second week of class at a very prestigious acting school in New York City. The professor, a critically acclaimed playwright and working actor in theatre, film, and television, was answering our questions at the end of the period. Timidly, I raised my hand.

"I got called back to read for a part in an upcoming production," I said. "But instead of the role I had auditioned for, the casting director wants me to read for the part of the antagonist. I'm not sure how to go about this, because I can't relate to the character. On the other hand, it's a big project and I don't want to lose out on the opportunity of getting seen. How do I get myself in the frame of mind to read for this part?"

Our professor took a moment to answer as we held our collective breath for his response; firstly, the man really knew his craft so anything he said to us was worth its weight in gold; secondly, this was a scenario that we'd all been through at some point but that few actors liked to admit was a real challenge. Most people cast themselves as the good guy, the hero, the protagonist of the story that is their life; and actors are no different. So when we're called back to read for the role of the bad guy, our first response is excitement followed up by immediate disappointment and self-loathing, convinced that our high school drama teacher had been right all along (that we are in fact fakes and posers, and that we'll never make it and should just give it up already). Once we're done singing our spiritual about always being the bridesmaid, yada yada, we're left with the business of figuring out how to read for a character that has seemingly zero redeeming qualities.

He cleared his throat. "It's important to remember that even bad guys love something. Maybe it's something in their past, before whatever happened to make them a bad guy, happened. Put yourself in their shoes, because it's really not hard to do. We're all just people, with the same needs, wishes…desires. If you can keep that in mind, you can play any character. Even a monster." And suddenly, I knew exactly where my villain was coming from. I was even rooting for her.

It's a common technique in marriage counseling as well, where dueling couples are encouraged to argue from the other person's point of view, to defend each other's positions. This can work wonders almost immediately because suddenly you understand exactly what your partner is referring to when they accuse you of being demanding, or disconnected, or aloof. You realize that they're not annoying you on purpose – ok, ok, maybe they *are*, but their intentions are understandable, even to you. Seeing things from the other person's perspective can really help you understand where you're going wrong; sometimes what we think we're putting out there is totally not what's being perceived. By arguing an opposing viewpoint once in a while, we gain valuable insight and learn to challenge our own perceptions;

we also get to see ourselves from a different point of view, a priceless perspective, because how we *think* others see us and how others *actually* see us are usually two wildly different versions of ourselves.

Most people act according to what their conscience tells them is the right thing to do, even when the results don't quite turn out the way they planned. This phenomenon is a popular theme in art, especially film. *King Kong, Frankenstein*, and *The Green Mile* all come to mind, but one of the best examples of this is Joel Schumacher's 1993 masterpiece, *Falling Down*. Michael Douglas plays an unemployed defense contractor trying to make his way across town to visit his young, estranged daughter on her birthday; instead, he's met with assorted social ills that create roadblocks – literally and figuratively – to his well-intentioned goal. At the end of the story, coming face to face with law enforcement and sure demise, he asks the heartbreaking question:

> Am I the bad guy? How'd that happen? I did everything they told me to.

I get chills.

First, Seek to Understand

Now, that's not to say that we're going to necessarily agree with the other person's actions, but at least we can see where they're coming from and how we may have contributed to any misunderstanding. Many times, people associate one thing with another when the two are completely unrelated, usually because they tend to react before they've given themselves a chance to think things through. For example, I often debate on political forums on Facebook, where the issue of President Obama's recent Executive Order in reference to immigration was a hot topic. The anti-Obama faction was outraged at POTUS' decision, calling it "amnesty" and warning of the economic avalanche that was sure to befall the U.S. as the floodgates would now be flung open to allow in every low-skilled worker from Latin America. Amnesty, they claimed, would be the end of our way of life. I very calmly reminded everyone that:

> Amnesty has been granted before; Ronald Reagan did it in the 1980's. Everybody relax.

This set off a firestorm of expletives from those folks who consider Reagan to have been more of a deity than merely a prior leader of the free world. They pointed out, repeatedly, that Reagan was working *with* the Congress, unlike Obama, who had overstepped Congress to push for amnesty. So then I calmly pointed out that I hadn't said anything to the contrary, but that the results – amnesty for illegals in the U.S. – were exactly the same. Obama did it alone, and Reagan did it with Congress' help, but at the end of the day both men pushed for the same agenda, which was all I was saying.

At this point, the anti-Obama faction changed their position – it wasn't the amnesty that was necessarily disturbing, it was the fact that it was an Executive Order, done without cooperation, without the blessing of Congress. After all, hadn't Senator Ted Cruz (considered by these good people to be a reincarnated cross between John Wayne and Thomas Jefferson – in other words, a "real patriot") accused Obama of "lawlessness" in a Wall Street Journal op-ed? And wouldn't Cruz know of what he spoke when he said:

Of all the troubling aspects of the Obama presidency, none is more dangerous than the president's persistent pattern of lawlessness, his willingness to disregard the written law and instead enforce his own policies via executive fiat.

It seemed to me that Senator Cruz either didn't remember recent history, or perhaps that he was never taught it; either way, I asked:

"So, it's not that President Obama offered amnesty that bothers you, am I hearing you right? It's the *way* he did it, through Executive Order. Am I hearing you correctly?"

"Yes, of course," True American Hero replied. "That's the problem right there. He's steamrolling over Congress. It's not constitutional; he's not the King."

I reminded everyone that Ronald Reagan had enacted 381 Executive Orders while in office, and that George W. Bush had enacted 291. Even my all-time favorite president, Theodore Roosevelt, had enacted a stunning 1,081 Executive Orders during his tenure. But President Obama? He had enacted just 193. The numbers didn't support Senator Cruz' accusations, so...what *was* the problem here?

"A federal judge [in Pennsylvania, mind you] ruled that Obama's executive order is unconstitutional, so this is different."

Different? Or kinda like the same as when Abraham Lincoln suspended habeas corpus in 1861 through executive order, even though Supreme Court Chief Justice Roger

Taney, serving in his role as a federal circuit judge, ruled that it was unconstitutional (Ex Parte Merryman)? Lincoln ignored this decision, and Congress didn't contest it. It actually sounds quite familiar, not "different" at all.

Which is when I got accused of advocating for something called "Big Government," which seems to depend a lot on who is actually in power. If it's "your" party, then somehow it's necessary and ok; but when it's the other guy doing it, suddenly it's a monarchy. I asked anyone to please provide where I had said that, anywhere. Because I wasn't advocating anything, simply pointing out that if amnesty is the problem, then it's a problem that has been created by members of both parties. If the problem is POTUS' use of Executive Orders, then again, both parties are guilty as charged. And that was my only point – that these problems aren't inherent traits of any one party, but innate in the Government *as a whole*. Because there is only *one* Government, no matter how many times its members attempt to cleverly market themselves as "two parties."

Revelation

At this point, the conversation finally shifted from a blame-game to a conversation about the impact of amnesty on the economy and on immigrants that came here legally, about why the immigration system in the U.S. is failing, and started a brainstorming session to figure out where changes could be made to help facilitate and control legal immigration to the states. Then came the defining question: Why punish the illegals, while allowing the Corporations that hire them – especially those in Big Agra and the food industry – to get off scott-free? After all, if these large industries weren't hiring illegals, illegals certainly wouldn't have a reason to come here in droves. And yet, these big agricultural firms have gotten away with their lawlessness for years, with little repercussion – why?

According to Politifacts, although President Obama has cracked down on employers that hire illegal labor, auditing more than 8,000 in 2009 (up from just 503 in 2008 during George W. Bush's tenure) and sanctioning major employers (including a $1 million fine against Abercrombie and Fitch), he doesn't hold the highest record on final orders against employers, which hit higher numbers between 1992 and 1998, peaking at 1,063 final orders in 1992 (U.S. Immigration Statistics Yearbook). So he holds the record for audits, but not for bringing cases to prosecution. Why not?

Now we were finally onto something that made sense and that we all agreed on; the Government itself is attracting illegals by allowing behemoth Corporations to hire them, simple as that. If you don't want an influx of low-skilled illegal immigrants in the U.S., then you have to push for the prosecution of the Corporations that hire them. Blaming the immigrant isn't going to resolve this issue, that much was clear. The immigration problem is caused by the collusion between the Government and its Corporate friends.

By switching sides and trying to see thing from your opponent's point of view, the real drivers behind the challenges we face rise up to the fore and can then be addressed. Because at the end of the day, aren't the "We the People" really just on the same side...?

The Politics of Geography

I'd like to point out here that geography plays a huge part in shaping the worldview of nations and of the individuals that live within them. The United States has

135

had the geographical good fortune to be separated by two vast oceans from the rest of the world and all its problems, as well as from any real threat from a foreign power. Our only neighboring nations – Canada and Mexico – pose no imminent danger, neither are these states radically different from our own, ideologically speaking; we don't wage wars with them, we trade. While our geographical protections are amazing assets and we are very fortunate to have them, these factors are also what keep the vast majority of Americans in the dark about international politics and global relations. Many Americans firmly believe that what works for us should work for others, and most are greatly bewildered as to why some nations just can't seem to get their act together.

But think about it. Because we didn't have a great abundance of gold and silver on our territory, the U.S. was largely left alone to develop without suffering the plundering tendencies of imperialist European states; but of course, not all nations were as lucky, and the repercussions of how these resource-rich territories were colonized are still being felt today. Because our nation wasn't built on religious dogma, we have a difficult time understanding the religious wars in Africa and the Middle East; the atrocities that are committed by the "faithful," and the petulant, almost infantile attitudes of leaders who seemingly would rather squander their own resources (and ours) fighting enemy "tribes" than to come to common-sense concessions that would help them put the past behind them and catch up to the rest of the developed world. Because Americans generally prize practicality above ideology, we don't understand why other nations won't embrace the many benefits of pragmatism. Because we don't live beneath the constant menace of war, we are lulled into a false confidence that we can afford to ignore global economics, how international finance works, and how our nation's foreign policy affects the rest of the planet and boomerangs back on us.

Geography also affects how we Americans understand our domestic politics as well; where we live – the size of the population, the demographics, the climate, the natural resources that our state either has or lacks – dictates what we feel most passionately about, the solutions we come up with to deal with the challenges we face, and also, how we regard the citizens in the rest of the country. Of course there are core beliefs that we all share, such as equality before the law, the right to express ourselves freely, the right to protect ourselves from harm, and our right to privacy; but other beliefs, such as what to do about education, marriage equality, immigration, and energy vary wildly depending on where our home state is located on the map.

Americans who live in high-powered big cities with large, multicultural populations have different needs than Americans who live in small, rural towns with less people. Our perspectives differ depending on where we're standing, and unless we have the opportunity to travel and live in different parts of the country, we have to learn to listen to one another if we're going to get a better perspective of what's going on around the nation. Understanding how the differences in our geography shape our respective political beliefs can help us understand each other and appreciate the value of what each of us brings to the table.

It may seem to big-city folks that small-town Americans are ignorant and inflexible, just like it may seem to small-town Americans that big-city folks are disloyal to our founding principles, and unpatriotic; but these broad opinions ignore the unique strengths and talents of both groups. Small-town Americans may not have a lot of worldly experience and they may not adapt as quickly to new realities, but no one can deny that they truly love this nation and fight hard to protect the foundations that this nation was built on. Big-city Americans may not have the same loyalty to old-fashioned ideals and they may be too quick to abandon them in the name of progress, but no one can deny that their efforts have improved the living conditions in our nation and have ensured that all Americans can equally enjoy the same rights, liberties, and benefits of living in this great country.

When we switch sides, we can understand why gun rights are of major concern to small-town Americans, for example; guns are part of their culture, and most of them grew up hunting with their families for sport, for food, and for familial bonding. Their right to bear arms is usually what's kept them safe from outside forces historically, and they prize their autonomy and their ability to protect their property and ones they love. Likewise, we can understand why gun control is a major issue for big-city folks; with populations numbering in the millions comes higher rates of crime and mental illness, and with the stresses of big-city living added to the mix, it's easy to see why big-city folks might seek greater gun restrictions in order to keep their streets and crowded public spaces safe.

The same goes for education; small-town Americans may prefer to home-school their kids because they have the time to do it, and also because they know most of their neighbors and can work together to create an alternative to public education. Big-city folks, on the other hand, may not have the luxury of staying home to teach their kids the basics; they depend on a responsive, effective public school system to educate their children while they themselves are out in the world making a living. Also, with so many people residing in one area, big-city folks are highly interdependent and realize that a well-educated population keeps crime down and helps everyone get along better, so education is vital to living harmoniously in a large society.

Fracking might seem like a great idea if you live in a state that produces the chemicals and equipment used in the process, but not so much if you live in a community whose water supply is being poisoned by the chemicals used to extract natural gas from deep within the earth. Factory-farming, the mass production of meat products and produce under more than questionable circumstances, might seem like a vile way to feed a nation, unless you live in a community where Big Agra controls the means of production; if farming is the only way you know to support your family, you're going to have to do it the Big Pharma way, or not do it at all.

The Role of States Rights

These differences are why states rights are important; because local citizens know what their needs are better than anyone else, they are also best suited to determine what constitutes meaningful policy within their territories through their local Government. However, can you imagine the chaos that would ensue if every time we crossed a state line the rules were drastically and fundamentally changed? There are certain issues that affect us all as the citizens of the nation and that should not be left up to individual states to decide because if certain standards are not upheld consistently across state borders, either the nation will suffer losses, or individuals won't be represented equally before the law. Or both. Economic issues such as education, energy, immigration, and marriage equality are matters that affect every American both as individuals and as members of the larger collective. Policies in one state create ripple effects in all of the others; and although 'one size fits all' doesn't apply to every law, I think we can agree that there are certain issues that aren't really up for debate. Matters like equality before the law, like a strong, healthy, and educated labor force, freedom of speech, and safe food production.

When we discuss politics with other People let's switch sides for a minute by keeping in mind where they're literally coming from; let's remember that their viewpoints, although different from ours, weren't arrived at from living on a different planet but from living right here in the good ole' U.S. of A. Let's consider the validity of their arguments according to the realities that they face in their home states. Let's also keep in mind the many valuable contributions that their efforts make to the country as a whole. Instead of writing each other off, let's reach out and determine where our common interests lie, and how we can work together to ensure that our rights and interests aren't sacrificed in an effort to meet our needs.

VII. Play nice.

"Separate an individual from society, and give him an island or a continent to possess, and he cannot acquire personal property. He cannot be rich. So inseparably are the means connected with the end, in all cases, that where the former do not exist the latter cannot be obtained. All accumulation, therefore, of personal property, beyond what a man's own hands produce, is derived to him by living in society; and he owes on every principle of justice, of gratitude, and of civilization, a part of that accumulation back again to society from whence the whole came."

‑ Thomas Paine, *"Agrarian Justice"*

"We the People." ‑ Preamble, *The Constitutional of the United States*

You love your country, that's obvious. If you didn't, you wouldn't be reading this book. You wouldn't spend the time and energy to stay politically aware and involved in your community, your nation, and in the world at large; you wouldn't debate the issues, and you wouldn't volunteer your talents to those causes that you believe are part of the solution. There is no doubt that you, my friend, are a patriot.

Play nice.

The beauty of the U.S. is that although we are a nation of immigrants, each of us with our own distinct perspectives, coming from many different backgrounds and individual experiences, it's our impenetrable, common belief in the right to life, liberty, and the pursuit of happiness that binds us all together. Through our united efforts, we are stronger, smarter, more efficient, and better able to address the issues that we face as a People. When we all work together, we have more resources and more answers, more perspectives and more solutions. But when we use our time and efforts to attack one another over our perceived differences, we weaken our bond and diminish our options. A weakened People are unable to defend their rights, or to work to promote their own interests. A weakened People are at the mercy of Government and Industry, who have learned long ago how to effectively cooperate with each other to promote their own agendas.

The expansion of social media into nearly every aspect of our private and public lives doesn't have to be something to fear; it can be a vital tool, a power to be harnessed. Never before in the history of mankind have we been able to instantly access the support, wisdom, and vitality of thousands of People that we would otherwise never cross paths with. While this is inspiring, it can also backfire on us if we don't remember to play nice.

Playing nice doesn't mean agreeing with everything everyone else has to say, but it does mean showing mutual respect, some common decency, and the foresight to take a minute before lambasting someone simply because we disagree with them. A good tactic to use before you post that scathing remark on Facebook is to ask yourself – would you respond as forcefully, as rudely, if you were face-to-face with the person you are addressing? Would you respond with the same blunt words and terse expressions if you were speaking to someone who could potentially open a window of opportunity for you, someone who was a potential customer, or who was vetting you for a new position, a loan, a part, or a publishing deal?

If we were all connected by six degrees of separation before the full integration of social media in our lives, imagine how much more we are all connected to each other today. Everyone you know right now is connected to literally thousands of other people through their social media networks, and the benefits of these contacts are yours to tap into and enjoy, and to reach out to and grow from, unless you screw it up and burn hundreds if not thousands of bridges with just a few stupid and insulting comments. In our digitally connected world, everyone is well served by playing nice because once it's up on the Internet, it's accessible to everyone, forever. Don't let one minute of frustration haunt you for a lifetime.

Face-to-Face Politiquette

These are easy to recognize (usually), because people give us a ton of non-verbal clues as to what effect we're having on them as we're having it, so we're better able to assess when we should pull back if we're going too far, or press forward if we see they're receptive to what we're saying. However, there are many ways to improve our face-to-face interactions; here are a few pointers to keep in mind:

1. **Smile.** Like with dogs, people respond primarily to how you say something rather than to what you are actually saying. Smiling relaxes you and them; it lowers defenses. Discourse should be a sport, not

a war. Keeping it friendly helps you achieve your goal of collecting intel (different perspectives, new information), garnering cooperation, and creating a solution.

2. **Connect commonalities.** If they're debating with you, clearly you already share similar interests - politics, economics, foreign relations, etc. Zone in on your common pursuits and establish those first. Where'd you grow up? Where'd you go to school? What hobbies and sports teams do you both root for? Establishing your commonalities early on will help you both stay more receptive to what the other has to say. The differences in our opinions are easier to navigate and discuss when we know that the person on the other side understands us, that they know where we're "coming from." Get to know your audience *before* the conversation turns towards politics or the economy; needless to say, the worst time to find out you're debating your boss' husband is *after* you've spent 20 minutes obnoxiously bullet-pointing just how horribly wrong he is on all of the issues.

3. **Stick to the subject.** Do not make the debate personal; yes, connect with your opponent on a personal level to establish commonalities, but when discussing the issues, leave the personal stuff out of it. No personal attacks.

4. **Clarify your intent.** Problems are caused by many factors, not just one cause; intelligent people understand this. Blame-games are intellectually

lazy and are counterproductive; they obscure the matter at hand, they don't clarify the issue. Avoid this by stating your intent clearly and without finger wagging; instead of "Deadbeats on welfare are sucking this nation dry," how about, "Our high rate of underemployment/outsourcing due to international trade agreements/need for entitlement reform, is keeping too many Americans dependent on social services. It's a conundrum, but there's gotta be a way to solve it. What's your take on this?" By stating your intent clearly – to find a solution to the burden of social services on the taxpayers by stemming the need for social services to begin with, as opposed to passing judgment on a diverse demographic with distinct circumstances – and by asking for the other person's input, you take the contention out of the debate and open up the discussion to include more options and different points of view, increasing your chances of having a fruitful debate.

5. **Admit when you're wrong.** Every one makes mistakes: when yours are pointed out to you, just admit them graciously and move on. Don't overreact and don't get defensive; you're not perfect and no one is expecting you to be. Relax. Don't waste time defending your position if it was made in error; sacrificing your credibility in favor of your ego is just dumb.

6. **Let them save face.** Don't embarrass someone because they've made an error, or because they've come up with unworkable solutions based on bad

information. Correct them but don't berate them because berating them won't get them to accept new information and revise themselves, it will just force them to hang onto their error all the more tightly. "I used to think that way too, until I read that..." is a good way to ease any tension when pointing out an error.

7. **Don't go away mad.** Debate should open up opportunity and foster a foundation for solutions, it shouldn't close doors for you or the person you're engaging. Keep this goal in mind before walking away; you should still be able to shake hands at the end of your discussion. Just because someone doesn't accept the validity of an argument today, doesn't mean that they never will; often, people just need some time to mull things over. When you end the debate on a friendly note, you allow them – and yourself – that time, and increase the chances that you'll be able to collaborate with that person and combine your resources to create viable solutions in the future.

Online Politiquette

The rules for online discourse are similar to those for face-to-face debates, but they're easier to forget because the Internet makes us all feel as if we were anonymous somehow, or that the conversation isn't "real" – all the more reason to tread lightly. There is literally no information someone couldn't uncover about you if they really wanted to, no matter how "private" you think your accounts are. Use the following guidelines and avoid some grief:

1. **No name-calling.** Call people by their names, whichever ones *they* use on social media; don't baptize them with new names they haven't chosen for themselves. Calling people "idiot," "moron," "sweetie," "honey," "libber," "RINO," "Republicrat," "Commie," "Paul-bot," racial slurs, gender slurs, etc., says more about you then it does about them. On the flip side, if you get called a name, don't take it personally; give the offender the benefit of the doubt. They're probably just lashing out because they've grown used to "debating" that way online. You can calmly point out that you haven't insulted them, and that you'd appreciate that same respect in turn. I've used this tactic myself plenty of times and I haven't come across too many people who don't respond well to it. If you encounter someone who keeps attacking you and won't focus on the topic at hand, just block them; don't return the favor, because that will only diminish your own credibility and foster ill will among everyone else. Plus, it's just not worth the aggravation.

2. **No threats.** Surprisingly, some people are still stupid enough to make threats on Facebook, Twitter, etc., without taking into account the repercussions – and there are many. If you feel that you're becoming emotionally unhinged during an online discussion (which is weird, because it's really not that serious), you can always choose to ignore the conversation; no one is *forcing* you to respond to a Facebook or Twitter comment. You can always type, "Gotta go, ttyl," (*ttyl = talk to you later) and leave it at that. There is no reason, ever, to threaten someone over

a debate. If anyone threatens you, take a screen shot of the conversation (including the top part of your screen which includes your name, the date, and the time) and save it in the "Pictures" file on your computer. Report the person, and block them. If it comes down to it, at least you have proof of the exchange.

3. **Keep it small.** THERE'S NOTHING MORE ANNOYING THAN A PERSON WHO RESPONDS IN ALL CAPS AND EXCLAMATION POINTS!!!!!! It's synonymous with yelling your head off, and we all know what happens to drama queens – they're ignored. If you have a point to make, then make it; neither expletives nor caps are going to help you get your point across, nor will they validate an argument that's poorly made.

4. **Keep it short.** Nobody appreciates it when you copy/paste long comments on a thread, and trust me no one is going to read them, so save your energy. Again, if you have a point you should be able to make it succinctly; if you're rambling, you probably don't have one.

5. **No link/meme bombing.** I love funny memes; they're fun, they get to the point quickly, and they can break up tension. I enjoy them even when I don't agree with them, but that's because I value a good laugh over fact-raging any day. However, when you bomb a thread with link upon link (which nobody reads) and meme after meme, people will switch

you off. Moderation is the key to effectiveness; keep memes and links to a minimum and your audience will be more apt to check them out.

6. **No expletives.** Show some courtesy for your audience and use real language to get your point across. Expletives put people on the defensive and they confuse your message; a lot of meaning and inflection gets lost when reading text vs. real conversation, and expletives can have really bad consequences if they're taken in an unintended way. Avoid all that as much as you can. If you absolutely must use an expletive to get your message across (not sure what message that would be, but let's just roll with it) use an acronym, a euphemism, sarcasm, one of these: %#@*&, or be creative and make up your own expletive that everyone will understand but no one will get offended by. For example:
    a. Bullsnap. This is one of my faves, feel free to use it.
    b. Arse. Unless you're a Brit, is this even a real word? I think not.
    c. WTF
    d. GTOH
    e. STFU
    f. Also, use emoticons. You get the idea. ;)

7. **Families/kids are off-limits.** Do NOT troll someone's Facebook pictures and LinkedIn accounts just to collect data to use against them in a debate; that is unacceptable and vile behavior. You're debating them on the issues; their families, careers, and especially their kids, have absolutely

nothing to do with any valid, logical argument you could possibly make. It's a low blow and I'm sure you wouldn't want this behavior to boomerang on you, so don't do it. Remember the Golden Rule: people are much more apt to respect your privacy if you respect theirs first.

Here's a fun exercise...

Scroll through your online history and read your past posts; do you recognize yourself? Do any of them make you cringe? Do you wish you could go back and delete them all, even though it really wouldn't matter, because once your posts are out there anyone and everyone has access to them? We all vent, but is venting *all* you're doing? What is the story that your posts and comments are telling? What version of yourself are you putting out into the cyberverse?

The doozy: Pretend for a minute that you aren't yourself; if you only had your comments and posts to go on, would you want to be friends with yourself? Would you take yourself seriously? Would you consider yourself to be a credible source, and your arguments valid?

If the answer is "no," fix that. Ask yourself why not, and be specific. Pin down those qualities that would turn you away and write them down, because only then will you be able to work on avoiding these pitfalls and revising your approach.

An Attitude of Gratitude

Egoism is rampant across the U.S., in fact, we're known worldwide for it (refer to the litany of overbearing American celebrities here). This is especially true in politics, where most Americans walk around with blinders on, working hard to push their own political agendas while stubbornly refusing to see things from anyone else's point of view. Then there are those who "sell out" and abandon a worthy cause once they've achieved success in their lives; finally having their own needs met, they conveniently forget the needs of others and choose to ignore injustices instead of using their improved status as a tool to affect change. Powerful people and celebrities who fund charitable causes and humbly bring awareness to the plight of others often get criticized for doing so, which is ridiculous; by spreading their good fortune around so that it benefits others, they serve us all. A lot has been written about the "me, me, me" generation, with some sources citing Baby Boomers as the most narcissistic brood this nation has ever produced, and others claiming that that honor goes to Millennials; but I'd like to point out that if we don't get our act together and figure out how to cooperate soon, the repercussions will be such that it's not gonna matter *who's* to blame.

Esprit de corps is the "team spirit" that inspires enthusiasm, devotion, and strong regard for the honor of the group. It's the can-do attitude that allows teams to face their opponents and claim victory, and also, to overcome defeat, regroup, and plan a winning strategy to take back with them onto the field. No one wins them all, but *without* esprit de corps, you can't win any of them, period. Unfortunately, Americans have forgotten this truism, or they've abandoned it, preferring to pretend instead that "every man for himself" would be a better strategy for our nation moving forward. However, "every man for himself" didn't build this country – *that* took immense effort and sacrifice from countless people, all working together for the benefit of the whole.

Where there is exchange and common interests, there is community. No man is an island; no man accomplishes anything notable by himself, but through the cooperation and efforts of hundreds if not thousands of other people. Every major human achievement has come about through the power of collective efforts; not one major human creation was produced or distributed in a bubble, not one human feat was reached alone. Even something as mundane as the breakfast that you eat in the morning requires immense efforts from countless other human beings just to bring it to your table.

Accepting this reality is the first step to understanding one's place in the world and in history, and furthermore, to find a purpose and a gratifying meaning to life. That you pay for a service doesn't mean that the person providing it is suddenly undeserving of further appreciation, that they don't warrant any other type of acknowledgement for their work; there are countless ways in which their efforts can never be repaid with just money. For example, even if you had the ability to pay for a surgery in full, it doesn't mean that you shouldn't recognize the sacrifice and hard work that went into that particular medical advancement which therefore made it available to you. What good would your money have done you if the life-saving surgery wasn't possible because it had yet to be developed, or because you couldn't find a donor willing to think of someone other than his or herself?

Neither does your money "pay for" the compassionate way in which your surgeon explained your condition to you, nor her thoughtful bedside manner, nor her patience in dealing with your family when they barraged her with dozens of questions about your condition; all of these are repaid with sincere regard, because at the end of the day, there really *are* things that money just cannot buy. I speak from experience; my daughter, the love of my life, had a health scare not long ago. Needless to say, our family was devastated, not to mention my daughter, who is a bright, beautiful young woman just starting out in life. Thankfully, after extensive blood tests, biopsies, sonograms, and CT scans, it ended up being something completely harmless and reversible; but the kindness, perseverance, and diligence generously granted to us by her surgeon, the nurses, and the technicians involved can never be repaid. Our family will be forever grateful to Dr. Alan Beitler, Margaret Buckley, and the staff at Keller Hospital.

Living in gratitude for the awe-inspiring contributions of our fellow man is a necessary component to living a full, rewarding life, and it should inspire us to contribute in kind. We're only here for a very limited amount of time, and there is nothing more satisfying then knowing that although short, our life mattered; that we have left something valuable, significant, and beneficial behind for our families, our communities, our country, and if we're *very* lucky, for the world. When we live a life that is of service to others, expanding the reach and scope of our efforts and good will, we don't diminish our strength – we magnify it. The power of our endeavors and our resources grows with the number of people that they serve. When we hoard our gifts, resources, and talents to serve the least amount of people possible, our efforts lack the conditions they need to grow and thrive; our potential contributions die with us. And since we can't take any of it with us…what's the point in keeping it to ourselves?

True Value

Nothing great has ever been accomplished in this world that didn't serve the needs of the greater community; in fact, the very value of every human achievement, every revered work of art, technological invention, discovery, and even political occurrence, is judged in direct proportion to how many people were able to benefit from it, and to what degree. Considering that we have been blessed with membership to the greatest society in the history of civilization, a nation that has afforded more rights, more liberties, and more opportunities to more people than any that came before it, you would think that we as Americans would enjoy a very strong sense of esprit de corps, pulling together for the good of the team; if this has ever been true of our nation, it's not anymore. Too many of us have abandoned this winning spirit in favor of divisiveness, contention, and pettiness. Herein lies a huge contradiction: how can we claim to love our country, while at the same time, despising her People?

I realize that not everyone was raised under the same conditions, and that sometimes people who weren't lucky enough to grow up in a home where generosity and teamwork were practiced, honored, and encouraged have a difficult time extending themselves for the benefit of others, especially for People they don't even know. But considering the current state of the nation and the contention and ill-will behind it, we're all going to have to make a concerted effort to overcome our own insecurities and fears and to learn to work with our fellow Americans if we're going to promote our shared interests. A nation is just an expanded neighborhood, it's a unit in which every member is integral and each has the ability to help the team win – or lose. It's a horribly worn-out cliché but the honest truth is that we *are* only as strong as our weakest link; instead of allowing the powers that be to exploit these weaknesses to their own benefit, why not unite our efforts in order to strengthen these weak spots?

Today's Main Event: The Past v. The Future

Some Americans today pine for a time gone by, a time when they think the nation was better off socially and economically. This is absurd to most everyone else because obviously time travel is impossible and so yearning for reversal is futile; but actually, the urge to regress is a normal phenomenon in human nature and quite understandable, especially during times of great change because change means delving into uncharted territory. Some people consider the unknown exciting and ripe with new opportunities; but for others, it inspires fear and a desire to return to more familiar surroundings, even if the memory of those preferable surroundings might not square with reality.

Politicians know this and they exploit it their advantage, promising to "take the nation back" by duplicating the political policies that existed in the past; but of course, this is pure drivel. Behind every seemingly successful era in our past are a myriad of unknown factors that facilitated that success which cannot be repeated unless we had a flying DeLorean, and maybe not even then. If instead of listening to the empty rhetoric of politicos we'd take the time to actually study our history, we'd realize that much of our nostalgia is flawed because it's built around ignorance,

Play nice.

mythology, and half-truths, making it seem as if the past was somehow "better," when it actually wasn't; there are loads of unspoken failures throughout our history that are rarely conceded – in other words, things weren't as rosy and wonderful in the "good old days" as we sometimes like to pretend they were. Everybody knows this, but few people like to admit it.

Since the beginning of recorded civilization, every aging generation has believed wholeheartedly that things were better when *they* were young: that people were more virtuous somehow, that society was more decent, that their leaders were more apt and capable, and that the new generation is going to destroy the country. But *every* generation has had its fair share of challenges; every era has been marked with one type of struggle or another. The 1950s are romanticized by some Americans as the Golden Era of the U.S., a time when the nation's "Greatest Generation" reveled in economic strength and social homogeneity and harmony; but that was thanks to the destruction of Europe during WWII, and to the oppressive nature of the social and legal mores of the time: neither women, homosexuals, nor racial minorities were granted the same rights as healthy, straight, white males, so of course everyone else fell in line – they *had* to. Clearly, the 50s weren't so great for everybody; clearly, there were improvements that had to be made, and thankfully, they were. The U.S. of the present cannot be the U.S. of 1950 because the world is a different place today. We cannot relive the past, folks, nor should we want to; because in order to address our current needs we have to accept our *current* realities.

So how do we go forward without abandoning our founding principles, the very virtues that made our country great? Well, we might start by understanding how those principles apply to us today and how they serve our modern world. Considering that we can't go back in time, if a policy or tenet fails to address contemporary concerns, then maybe it *has* outlived its usefulness, and should be abandoned. If, on the other hand, a principle retains its usefulness, then the only way to keep that principle alive is to apply it in a way that expands its utility. If a policy or principle exists only to benefit a very small group of people, then either the number of beneficiaries must expand, or the policy must go. It's as simple as that.

Arguing over whether or not we should "take our country back" to a time long gone is absurd; it *can't* be done no matter what, so we're just wasting precious time fighting over nonsense at a moment when we can least afford to. Life is all about change; it's the normal order of things. Let's embrace change with enthusiasm and faith in ourselves; let's learn to work together with mutual respect and good will towards each other, so that the value of our founding principles won't be lost for good.

TO BE CLEAR: These Politiquette rules refer to debates that you have with other People, not debates that you have with ineffective or corrupt Government officials at town hall meetings and on Twitter; and they don't apply to those street and social media protests and boycotts that are mounted against predatory multi-national Corporations whose practices work against the interests of the People. When it comes to Government and Industry, hold their feet to the fire. Don't try to find "commonalities," because you have none. And of course you should never make threats, but don't be afraid of holding them accountable for their actions, for their associations, and for their policies, because these have the potential to diminish the welfare of the People. If the People won't call them out on their bullsh*t, no one will; remember that.

  With everyone else, play nice.

Epilogue

"Our greatest responsibility is to be good ancestors." ~ Jonas Salk

Whether you're an Independent fed up with your lack of representation in Washington, a moderate Democrat or Republican disappointed by the repeated failures and deceit of your party, or a Millennial whose disenchantment with our current system of Government has turned into apathy and an unwillingness to even try to make a difference, I hope that you now realize that you have options and the power to turn things around; in fact, We the People have an obligation to do so. America remains a world power and our Government's actions have far-reaching consequences all around the globe, repercussions that eventually boomerang back at us, affecting us all in ways we never imagined until it's too late.

But we can't change the current state of affairs until we realize that we're part of the problem: feeding into the fiction of the "two party" system and fighting amongst ourselves, even as our government creates policies to benefit its corporate friends at the expense of people everywhere. In the Information Age, the more we know, the more is expected of us; more so than in any other time in human history, we have the resources and the capacity to affect change and create a more just, balanced, and harmonious world. This isn't some Utopian dream, as the status quo would smugly like you to think; it's doable. Cynicism might protect you from disappointment, but it's not going to do anything else; abandon it. Use your time and energy to do your part. No one can do everything, but we can all do something; by contributing to the solution our collective efforts are amplified, and we all get closer to forming "a more perfect union."

Cuba

Considering my ancestry and the direct effect it's had both in forging my political passions and in shaping my political attitude, I would be remiss if I ended this work without addressing President Obama's call to lift the Cuban embargo, and where I stand on this issue in light of my unique perspective as a first-generation American of Cuban descent.

While I had the great privilege of being raised by an honorable generation of immigrants, the ugly truth is that the Cuban immigrants of today are nothing like the Cuban exiles of my parents' and grandparents' generation – hard working, productive, and often highly educated people from good families who migrated to the U.S. in the hope of rebuilding their lives in a nation that would reward their skills, talents, and efforts with a new opportunity to prosper. After living 60 years under the failed dictatorship of Fidel Castro – a welfare-state that has systemically de-incentivized work and education, and that has reduced the once-proud Cuban people into a desolate nation of prostitutes, swindlers, and petty criminals – Cubans that migrate to the U.S. today don't all necessarily come here to "reestablish" themselves, nor to take the opportunity to reinvent themselves in order to thrive and progress. Some come to duplicate and augment the lifestyle that they've become accustomed to: either living off of Government subsidies, or running illegal operations such as drug smuggling, human trafficking, and credit card fraud a in an American black market which they exploit in order to enrich themselves quickly before escaping back to Cuba. Due to arcane U.S. immigration laws concerning Cuban immigrants, some have been able to get away with it.

There is a lot of guilt involved when political refugees are compelled to leave their family and friends behind in a failing state in order to survive, especially when those exiles then get to enjoy a better life in a new country while their family and friends back home succumb to poverty, devastation, and injustice. This "survivor's guilt" is very common among the Cuban community of my parents' and grandparents' generation; although it's rarely spoken of, I believe it's a main driver behind their political activities in the United States.

Another driver is self-pity: when Cubans of my parents' and grandparents' generation immigrated to the U.S., they did so knowing that they'd probably never see their families again. Trips to Cuba were unheard of; phone calls to the island were exceedingly rare and oftentimes the connection dropped mid-sentence; letters – which took weeks if not months to arrive – were the most reliable mode of communication between themselves and their people back home, and many lost loved ones without ever having been able to say goodbye. Understandably, to see Cuban immigrants today reach the shores of the U.S. and then return to Cuba as visitors within six months feels like a slap in the face to the original Cuban exile community, who had to make so many painful sacrifices in comparison to today's Cuban immigrants, and who feel that the gravity of their plight has been forgotten in the name of progress.

A third driver is a feeling of betrayal: those who remember a prosperous and democratic Cuba feel saddened and outraged by the drastic change in their homeland and the devolution of its people. They blame Castro of course, but the U.S. as well, for not doing more to depose Castro and also for the many empty promises that ended up costing Cuban-American lives. Kennedy's disastrous failure during the Bay of Pigs debacle is probably the most famous event contributing to this contention, but more recently was the 1996 attack by Cuban military aircraft of two unarmed Brothers to the Rescue (BTTR) civilian aircraft, which killed four men as they penetrated Cuban airspace in an attempt to distribute anti-Castro leaflets on the island. The group's mission was compromised by three Cuban spies who infiltrated the organization and who were recently released by the Obama administration in exchange for the imprisoned American aid worker Alan Gross, adding even more fuel to an already explosive debate.

We can argue all day long about whether or not BTTR had been sufficiently warned of the dangers posed by continuously running these operations over the island's air space (this wasn't the first time BTTR had conducted similar activities); about whether or not the leaders of BTTR knew the risks but took them anyways; about whether or not the U.S. military was obligated to respond considering the repercussions (there was no response from the nearby U.S. Homestead Air Base); about where accountability lies and who is at fault for what. But at the end of the day, none of these arguments will change the basic driver behind the controversy – the older generation of Cuban immigrants feels wronged, and they want the U.S. to do something about it.

This is the environment in which President Obama has asked Congress to end the Cuban embargo. Clearly, there was no way this would go over well with Cuban-Americans of my parents' and grandparents' era because they are emotionally committed to seeing the Castro regime *destroyed*, once and for all. Where emotions trump reason, it's difficult if not impossible to successfully debate the issues by merely using statistics and data; pointing out that 50 years of the embargo has done nothing to depose Castro but has only decimated the island, diminished the standard of living for the people still residing there, and cost the U.S. economy billions in potential revenue will do absolutely nothing to sway their point of view. As much as I sympathize with them over the loss of their beloved homeland, I cannot support their ire, because ending the embargo is smart policy – both for the Cuban people, as well as for the U.S.

Ending the embargo allows the United States to gain a foothold in Cuba before the Castro regime comes to an end, as it inevitably must. This is a good preventative measure to protect our national security, as there is sure to be political turmoil on the island once Castro dies and leaves behind a power vacuum with many covert, interested parties vying to fill it. Considering that Cuba is only 90 miles off our coast, we'd be crazy not to look ahead and plan accordingly. Ending the embargo will also help establish free trade between the two nations, granting the U.S. direct access to the Cuban people, effectively giving the U.S. soft power in the region through the exportation of our cultural norms and mores. Thirdly, we'd be in a better position to negotiate extradition agreements, which would help us bring hundreds of wanted criminals to justice instead of allowing them safe haven on the island. And lastly, opening trade with Cuba would provide countless opportunities for both small businesses as well as large Industry in the American and Cuban markets, mutually raising the standard of living and expanding the revenue base for both countries.

After 50 years of failed policy and ideology, it's time to cut our losses and move on – that goes for everything across the board. Yes many died in Castro's "Revolution," but name a revolution in which there were no innocent casualties? Would continuing the cycle of death and injustice change the fate of those who have already suffered under the Castro regime? We can't flourish in the 21st Century if we're still stuck in the mentality of the past. This is not the 'Golden Era' of the 1950s, nor is it the Cold War Era; the New Millennium requires that we either adapt old policies so that they'll work for us today or abandon them altogether, boldly creating new solutions to address the unique challenges we currently face.

But the People can only achieve this by remaining open to possibilities, by actively seeking to understand things before creating judgments or formulating responses; and we can only do that if we're willing to abandon partisan labels, consider the facts with sober minds, and unite our efforts toward our common goal. That's how nature works, after all: by continuously correcting itself through trial and error, by continuously seeking to optimize its options for growth in its constant effort to perfect itself. In the natural world, rigidity and inflexibility spell death – the rule is, "adapt or die." The People – ALL People – would be wise to keep this in mind.

Those loud, often scary-sounding debates in our kitchen while I was growing up always ended with laughter and hugs good night between old friends and new neighbors who respected and loved one another. No they didn't always agree, but they knew that everyone was on the same side and working towards the same ends, even when their methods varied; and they appreciated the fact that although they each had different perspectives, everyone had something relevant to contribute to the group. In this way, they created an airtight bond that helped them achieve their objectives while raising a new generation of Americans who understood the value of mutual respect and cooperation amongst peers.

It's my most sincere hope that the American People will adapt this attitude today when addressing each other moving forward, abandoning old rhetoric and ideas that do nothing but hold us back and keep us down.

Our fate as a People in the New Millennium depends on it.

Works Cited & Resources

POLITRIX

Super Size Me. Dir. Morgan Spurlock. The Con; Kathbur Pictures, 2004. Film.

Burkeman, Oliver. "'Your Liver Is Turning into Pate'" *The Guardian.* Guardian News and Media, 15 July 2004. Web. 10 Feb. 2015.

The Associated Press. "McDonald's Phasing out Supersize Fries, Drinks." *Msnbc.com.* The Associated Press, 3 Mar. 2004. Web. 10 Apr. 2013.

"Full Menu Explorer." *McDonalds.com.* N.p., n.d. Web. 10 Apr. 2013.

Spurlock on Super Size Me. Perf. Morgan Spurlock. YouTube. YouTube, n.d. Web. 10 Feb. 2015.

Jeffrey Wigand, PhD. Interview by Mike Wallace. *60 Minutes Overtime.* Prod. Lowell Bergman. CBS, New York, 4 Feb. 1996. Television.

Centers for Disease Control and Prevention. "Trends in Current Cigarette Smoking Among High School Students and Adults, United States, 1965-2011." Web. N.p., n.d. 10 Feb. 2015. http://www.cdc.gov/tobacco/data_statistics/tables/trends/cig_smoking/index.htm

Centers for Disease Control and Prevention. "Current Cigarette Smoking Among Adults in the United States." Web. N.p., n.d. 10 Feb. 2015. http://www.cdc. gov/tobacco/data_statistics/fact_sheets/adult_data/ cig_smoking/

Food Chains. Dir. Sanjay Rawal. Illumine Group, Two Moons Production, 2014. Film.

Basic Concepts I: The Actors

Issa, Nai; Jacobson, Louis. "Congress Has 11% Approval Ratings but 96% Incumbent Reelection Rate, Meme Says." *Tampa Bay Times. Politifact.com.* 11 Nov. 2014. Web. 10 Feb. 2015.
http://www.politifact.com/truth-o-meter/ statements/2014/nov/11/facebook-posts/ congress-has-11-approval-ratings-96-incumbent-re-e/

"Small Donors Make Good Press, Big Donors Get You Reelected". *OpenSecrets.org.* N.p., n.d. Web. 10 Feb. 2015. https://www.opensecrets.org/resources/ dollarocracy/04.php

"Campaign for Accountability Files Lawsuit on Behalf of Investor Stephen Silberstein Against the SEC." *CampaignForAccountability.org.* N.p. 13 May 2015. Web. 14 Sept. 2015. http://campaignforaccountability. org/campaign-for-accountability-files-lawsuit-on- behalf-of-investor-stephen-silberstein-against-the-sec/

United States. Dept. of State. "Small Business in the United States." *About.com.* N.p., n.d. Web. 14 Sept. 2015. http://economics.about.com/od/smallbigbusiness/a/ us_business.htm

Kinzer, Stephen. *The Brothers: John Foster Dulles, Allen Dulles, and Their Secret World War.* New York: Times Books, 2013. Print.

Parry, Robert. *Ronald Reagan: Accessory to Genocide – Ex-Guatemalan Dictator Rios Montt Guilty of Mayan Genocide.* Consortium News, 11 May 2013. Global Research, 13 May 2013. Web. 14 Sept. 2015. http://www.globalresearch.ca/ronald-reagan-accessory-to-genocide-ex-guatemalan-dictator-rios-montt-guilty-of-mayan-genocide/5334855

Butler, Smedley D. *War is a Racket: The Antiwar Classic by America's Most Decorated Soldier.* 1935. Los Angeles: Feral House, 2003. Print.

Garofalo, Pat. "FLASHBACK: Corporations Used 2004 Tax Holiday to Repatriate Billions, Then Laid Off Thousands of Workers." *ThinkProgress.org* 14 May 2011. Web. 15 Sept. 2015.

"Citi to Cut 17,000 Jobs in Broad Overhaul." *New York Times* 11 April 2007, DealBook. Web. 15 Sept. 2015. http://dealbook.nytimes.com/2007/04/11/citi-to-cut-17000-jobs-in-broad-overhaul/

Basic Concepts II: The Free Market

Smith, Adam. *Inquiry into the Nature and Causes of the Wealth of Nations.* 1776. New York: Random House, 2003. Print.

Callahan, Ellena. "Stiglitz: The Invisible Hand is Invisible Because It Isn't There." The Roosevelt Institute. 2 Apr. 2012. Web. 15 Sept. 2015. http://www.nextnewdeal.net/rediscovering-government/stiglitz-invisible-hand-invisible-because-it-isnt-there

Marshall, Alfred. *Principles of Economics.* London: Palgrave Macmillian, 2014. Print.

Frizell, Sam. "Student Loans Are Ruining Your Life. Now They're Ruining the Economy, too." *Time* 26 Feb. 2014. Web. 15 Sept. 2015. http://time.com/10577/student-loans-are-ruining-your-life-now-theyre-ruining-the-economy-too/

Ellis, Blake. "40 Million Americans Now Have Student Loan Debt." *CNN Money* 10 Sept. 2014. Web. 15 Sept. 2015. http://money.cnn.com/2014/09/10/pf/college/student-loans/

United States. Dept. of Labor. *Bureau of Labor Statistics, Economic News Release.* 04 Sept. 2015. Web. 15 Sept. 2015. http://www.bls.gov/news.release/empsit.t15.htm

Efron, Louis. "Tackling the Real Unemployment Rate: 12.6%." *Forbes.com* 20 Aug. 2014. Web. 15 Sept. 2015. http://www.forbes.com/sites/louisefron/2014/08/20/tackling-the-real-unemployment-rate-12-6/

Chang, Jon M. "Mark Zuckerberg and Bill Gates Teach Coding Fundamentals to Computer Newbies." *ABCNews.com* 16 Oct. 2013. Web. 15 Sept. 2015. http://abcnews.go.com/Technology/mark-zucker-berg-bill-gates-teach-coding-fundamentals/story?id=20579277

Ryan, Julia. "American Schools vs. the World: Expensive, Unequal, Bad at Math." *The Atlantic* 03 Dec. 2013. Web. 15 Sept. 2015. http://www.theatlantic.com/education/archive/2013/12/american-schools-vs-the-world-expensive-unequal-bad-at-math/281983/

OECD. "United States." *OECD.org.* N.p., n.d. Web. 15 Sept. 2015. https://data.oecd.org/united-states.htm

Marcus, Jon. "New Analysis Shows Problematic Boom In Higher Ed Administrators." New England Center for

Investigative Reporting. *HuffingtonPost.com* 06 Feb. 2014. Web. 15 Sept. 2015. http://www.huffingtonpost. com/2014/02/06/higher-ed-administrators-growth_n_4738584.html

Federal Reserve Discount Window Payment System Risk. Web. 15 Sept. 2015. https://www.frbdiscountwindow.org

Butrymowicz, Sarah. "When Charter Schools Fail, What Happens to the Kids?" *The Hechinger Report* 31 Jan. 2012. Web. 15 Sept. 2015. http://hechingerreport.org/ when-charter-schools-fail-what-happens-to-the-kids/

I. Drop your labels.

"Rubio Says Immigration Plan Not Amnesty, Amid Conservative Scrutiny." *Fox News* 14 Apr. 2013. Web. 15 Sept. 2015. http://www.foxnews.com/ politics/2013/04/14/rubio-immigration-plan-not-amnesty-border-security-still-trigger-for/

Maloy, Simon. "Rubio's Desperate Immigration Lie: Rewriting His Own Record to Appease the Tea Party." *Salon* 22 July 2014. Web. 15 Sept. 2015. http://www.salon.com/2014/07/22/ rubios_desperate_immigration_lie_rewriting_his_ own_record_to_appease_the_tea_party/

"Rubio's Immigration Evolution." *FactCheck.org* 17 April 2013. Web. 15 Sept. 2015. http://www.factcheck. org/2013/04/rubios-immigration-evolution/

Gilens, Naomi. "New Justice Department Documents Show Huge Increase in Warrantless Electronic Surveillance." *ACLU.org* 27 Sept. 2012. Web. 15 Sept. 2015. https://www.aclu.org/blog/new-justice-department-documents-show-huge-increase-warrantless-electronic-surveillance?redirect=blog/

national-security-technology-and-liberty/
new-justice-department-documents-show-huge-increase

Lee, Carol E., Henderson, Nia-Malika. "Liberals Voice Concerns About Obama." *Politico.com* 08 Dec. 2012. Web. 15 Sept. 2015. http://www.politico.com/story/2008/12/liberals-voice-concerns-about-obama-016292

"US Government Admits to Killing Four American Citizens with Drones." *RT.com*. N.p. Web. 23 May 2013. http://www.rt.com/usa/us-government-drone-killing-660/

"Has Obama Gone Too Far With His Drone Policies?" *U.S. News & World Report*. N.p., n.d. Web. 15 Sept. 2015. http://www.usnews.com/debate-club/has-obama-gone-too-far-with-his-drone-policies

Smith, Yves. "Obama Wants to be the President Who Rolled Back the New Deal." *Alternet.org* 07 April 2013. Web. 15 Sept. 2015. http://www.alternet.org/news-amp-politics/obama-wants-be-president-who-rolled-back-new-deal

"$1.6B of Bank Bailout Went to Execs." *CBSNews.com* 21 Dec. 2008. Web. 15 Sept. 2015. http://www.cbsnews.com/news/16b-of-bank-bailout-went-to-execs/

United States. Congressional Oversight Panel. 09 Jan. 2009. Web. 15 Sept. 2015. http://web.archive.org/web/20110106141711/http://cop.senate.gov/documents/cop-010909-report.pdf

"U.S. Bailout Recipients Spent $114 Million on Politics." *Reuters* 04 Feb. 2009. Web. 15 Sept. 2015. http://www.reuters.com/article/2009/02/04/us-usa-bailout-lobbying-idUSTRE51377B20090204?feedType=RSS&feedName=politicsNews

Benjamin, Matthew., Harper, Christine. "Goldman, JPMorgan Won't Feel Effects of Executive-Salary Caps." *Bloomberg.com* 05 Feb. 2009. Web. 15

Sept. 2015. http://www.bloomberg.com/apps/news?pid=washingtonstory&sid=azVLk.22AkLI

Broes, Derek. "Why Should You Fear SOPA and PIPA?" *Forbes.com* 20 Jan. 2012. Web. 15 Sept. 2015. http://www.forbes.com/sites/derekbroes/2012/01/20/why-should-you-fear-sopa-and-pipa/

Johnson, Dave. "Upcoming Trans-Pacific Partnership Looks Like Corporate Takeover." *HuffingtonPost.com* 15 May 2013. Web. 15 Sept. 2015. http://www.huffingtonpost.com/dave-johnson/upcoming-trans-pacific-pa_b_3276855.html

Sutton, Maira. "TPP: Internet Freedom Activists Protest Secret Trade Agreement Being Negotiated This Week." *EFF.org* 14 May 2012. Web. 15 Sept. 2015. https://www.eff.org/tpp-another-backroom-deal

Clement, Benjamin. "Now Is the Time to Justifiably Protest the Trans-Pacific Partnership (TPP)." *EconomyInCrisis.org* 02 Feb. 2014. Web. 15 Sept. 2015. http://economyincrisis.org/content/now-is-the-time-to-justifiably-protest-the-trans-pacific-partnership-tpp

Armitage, Jim. "Big Tobacco Puts Countries on Trial as Concerns Over TTIP Deals Mount." *TheIndependent.co.uk* 21 Oct. 2014. Web. 15 Sept. 2015. http://www.independent.co.uk/news/business/analysis-and-features/big-tobacco-puts-countries-on-trial-as-concerns-over-ttip-deals-mount-9807478.html

Australian Fair Trade & Investment Network Ltd. "Australian High Court Rules Against Big Tobacco on Plain Packaging." N.d. Web. 15 Sept. 2015. http://aftinet.org.au/cms/node/519

Jolly, David. "Tobacco Giants Sue Britain Over Rules on Plain Packaging." *The New York Times* 22 May 2015. Web. 15 Sept. 2015. http://www.nytimes.

com/2015/05/23/business/international/tobacco-plain-packaging-philip-morris-british-american-cigarettes.html?_r=0

Reich, Robert B. *Saving Capitalism: For the Many, Not the Few.* New York: Knopf, 2015. Print.

Calmes, Jackie. "Trans-Pacific Partnership Is Reached, But Faces Scrutiny in Congress." *The New York Times.* 05 Oct. 2015. Web. 07 Oct. 2015. http://www.nytimes.com/2015/10/06/business/trans-pacific-partnership-trade-deal-is-reached.html?_r=0

Audley, John J.; Papademetriou, Demetrios G.; Polaski, Sandra; Vaughan, Scott. "NAFTA's Promise and Reality: Lessons From Mexico for the Hemisphere." *Carnegie Endowment for International Peace,* 2004. Web. 07 Oct. 2015. http://carnegieendowment.org/2003/11/09/nafta-s-promise-and-reality-lessons-from-mexico-for-hemishphere/278f

Barufaldi, Dan. "NAFTA's Winners and Losers." *Investopedia.* 23 July 2008. Web. 07 Oct. 2015. http://www.investopedia.com/articles/economics/08/north-american-free-trade-agreement.asp?adtest=article_page_v12_v2

McAuliff, Michael. "NAFTA Report Warns of Trade Deal Environmental Disasters." *Huffington Post.* 03 Nov. 2014. Web. 07 Oct. 2015. http://www.huffingtonpost.com/2014/03/11/nafta-environment_n_4938556.html

Maynard, James. "Bloomberg, Gates Fund Fight Against Big Tobacco in Developing World." *Tech Times* 18 March 2015. Web. 15 Sept. 2015. http://www.techtimes.com/articles/40654/20150318/bloomberg-gates-create-fund-help-developing-companies-fight-big-tobacco.htm

III. Share the facts.

Vergano, Dan. "Study: Emotion Rules the Brain's Decisions." *USA Today* 06 Aug. 2006. Web. 15 Sept. 2015. http://usatoday30.usatoday.com/tech/science/discoveries/2006-08-06-brain-study_x.htm

Wilson, Robert Evans Jr. "The Most Powerful Motivator." *Psychology Today* 23 Sept. 2009. Web. 15 Sept. 2015. https://www.psychologytoday.com/blog/the-main-ingredient/200909/the-most-powerful-motivator

Higgs, Robert. "Fear: The Foundation of Every Government's Power." *Independent Institute* 17 May 2005. http://www.independent.org/publications/article.asp?id=1510

Young, Angelo. "Cheney's Halliburton Made $39.5 Billion on Iraq War." *International Business Times* 20 March 2013. Web. 15 Sept. 2015. http://readersupportednews.org/news-section2/308-12/16561-focus-cheneys-halliburton-made-395-billion-on-iraq-war

Friedersdorf, Conor. "Dick Cheney, Rand Paul, and the Possibility of Malign Leaders." *The Atlantic* 09 Apr. 2014. Web. 22 Sept. 2015. http://www.theatlantic.com/politics/archive/2014/04/dick-cheney-rand-paul-and-the-possibility-of-malign-leaders/360372/

Fifield, Anna. "Contractors Reap $138B from Iraq War." *CNN*. N.d. Web. 22 Sept. 2015. http://www.cnn.com/2013/03/19/business/iraq-war-contractors/index.html

Foster, Peter. "Cost to US of Iraq and Afghan Wars Could Hit $6 Trillion." *The Telegraph* 29 Mar. 2013. Web. 22 Sept. 2015. http://www.telegraph.co.uk/news/worldnews/northamerica/usa/9961877/Cost-to-US-of-Iraq-and-Afghan-wars-could-hit-6-trillion.html

Bergen, Peter. "Target an American With Drones?" *CNN* 11 Feb. 2014. Web. 22 Sept. 2015. http://www.cnn.com/2014/02/11/opinion/bergen-target-american-with-drones/index.html

Wolff, Michael. "Wolff: Nobody's Neutral in Net Neutrality Debate." *USA Today* 22 Sept. 2014. Web. 22 Sept. 2015. http://www.usatoday.com/story/money/columnist/wolff/2014/09/21/net-neutrality-debate/15881687/

Cummings, Tucker. "Top 10 Best Set Top Boxes & Cable TV Alternatives." *Heavy.com* 19 May 2014. Web. 22 Sept. 2015. http://heavy.com/tech/2014/05/top-best-set-top-box-cable-tv-alternatives/

Seward, Zachary. "One Sentence and Six Charts to Explain Why Comcast is Buying Time Warner Cable." *QZ.com* 12 Feb. 2014. Web. 22 Sept. 2015. http://qz.com/176837/one-sentence-and-six-charts-explain-why-comcast-is-buying-time-warner-cable/

Masnick, Mike. "Ted Cruz Doubles Down On Misunderstanding the Internet & Net Neutrality, as Republican Engineers Call Him Out for Ignorance." *Techdirt.com* 17 Nov. 2014. Web. 22 Sept. 2015. https://www.techdirt.com/blog/netneutrality/articles/20141115/07454429157/ted-cruz-doubles-down-misunderstanding-internet-net-neutrality-as-republican-engineers-call-him-out-ignorance.shtml

Chappell, Bill. "FCC Approves Net Neutrality Rules for 'Open Internet.'" *NPR* 26 Feb. 2015. Web. 22 Sept. 2015. http://www.npr.org/sections/thetwo-way/2015/02/26/389259382/net-neutrality-up-for-vote-today-by-fcc-board

IV. Play fair.

Copi, Irving M. and Cohen, Carl. *Introduction to Logic.* New Jersey: Prentice Hall, 1998. Print.

Lizza, Ryan. "Romney's Dilemma." *The New Yorker* 06 June 2011. Web. 22 Sept. 2015.

U.S. Census Bureau. "Income, Poverty, and Health Insurance Coverage in the United States: 2010." Sept. 2011. Web. 22 Sept. 2015. http://www.census.gov/prod/2011pubs/p60-239.pdf

Himmelstein, David U.; Thorne, Deborah.; Warren, Elizabeth.; Woolhandler, Steffie. "Medical Bankruptcy in the United States, 2007: Results of a National Study". *The American Journal of Medicine* 05 June 2009. Web. 22 Sept. 2015. http://www.amjmed.com/article/S0002-9343(09)00404-5/abstract

"Obama: 'If you like your health care plan, you'll be able to keep your health care plan.'" *Politifact.com.* N.d. Web. 22 Sept. 2015. http://www.politifact.com/obama-like-health-care-keep/

Alonso-Zaldivar, Ricardo. "At Least 3.5 Million Americans Have Now Had Their Health Insurance Policies Canceled Thanks to Obamacare." *Business Insider* 03 Nov. 2013. Web. 22 Sept. 2015. http://www.businessinsider.com/at-least-35-million-americans-have-now-had-their-health-insurance-policies-canceled-thanks-to-obamacare-2013-11

Garret, B.; Kaestner, R. "Little Evidence of the ACA Increasing Part-Time Work So Far." *Robert Wood Johnson Foundation* Sept. 2014. Web. 22 Sept. 2015. http://www.rwjf.org/en/library/research/2014/09/little-evidence-of-the-aca-increasing-part-time-work-so-far.html

Shaw, Donny. "House Votes to End Antitrust Protections for Health Insurers." *OpenCongress.org* 24 Feb. 2010. Web. 22 Sept. 2015. https://www.opencongress.org/articles/view/1636-House-Votes-to-End-Antitrust-Protections-for-Health-Insurers

Jilani, Zaid. "Weiner Offends the GOP on House Floor: You're All 'Owned' by the 'Insurance Industry!'" *ThinkProgress.org* 24 Feb. 2010. Web. 22 Sept. 2015. http://thinkprogress.org/politics/2010/02/24/83800/anthony-weiner-subsidiary/

Brill, Steven. "Bitter Pill: Why Medical Bills Are Killing Us." *Time* 04 Apr. 2013. Web. 22 Sept. 2015. http://time.com/198/bitter-pill-why-medical-bills-are-killing-us/

Hancock, Jay. "Expert: Hospitals' 'Humongous Monopoly' Drives Prices High." *Kaiser Health News* 04 Mar. 2013. Web. 22 Sept. 2015. http://khn.org/news/expert-hospitals-humongous-monopoly-drives-prices-high/

Gaynor, Martin; Town, Robert. "The Impact of Hospital Consolidation – Update." *Robert Wood Johnson Foundation* June 2012. Web. 22 Sept. 2015. http://www.rwjf.org/content/dam/farm/reports/issue_briefs/2012/rwjf73261

Field, Robert. "Could Health Reform Create Hospital Monopolies?" *Philly.com* 17 Oct. 2013. Web. 22 Sept. 2015. http://www.philly.com/philly/blogs/healthcare/Could_health_reform_create_hospital_juggernauts.html

Pollack, Andrew. "Drug Goes From $13.50 a Tablet to $750, Overnight." *The New York Times* 20 Sept. 2015. Web. 23 Sept. 2015. http://www.nytimes.com/2015/09/21/business/a-huge-overnight-increase-in-a-drugs-price-raises-protests.html?_r=0

V. Change your mind.

Mr. Mom. Dir. Stan Dragoti. Twentieth Century Fox, 1983. Film.

Pratkanis, Anthony R. *The Science of Social Influence: Advances and Future Progress.* New York: Psychology Press, 2007. Print.

Perloff, Richard M. *The Dynamics of Persuasion: Communication and Attitudes in the 21st Century.* London: Routledge, 2002. Print.

VII. Switch sides.

King Kong. Dir. Merian C. Cooper, Ernest B. Schoedsack. RKO, 1933. Film.

Frankenstein. Dir. James Whale. Universal Pictures, 1931. Film.

The Green Mile. Dir. Frank Darabont. Warner Bros., 1999. Film.

Falling Down. Dir. Joel Schumacher. Warner Bros., 1993. Film.

Sherman, Amy. "Obama Holds Record for Cracking Down on Employers Who Hire Undocumented Workers, Says Wasserman Schultz." *Politico.* 03 July 2013. Web. 27 Sept. 2015. http://www.politifact.com/florida/statements/2013/jul/03/debbie-wasserman-schultz/obama-holds-record-cracking-down-employers-who-hir/

Epilogue

Kestin, Sally; O'Matz, Megan; Maines, John; Eaton, Tracey. "Plundering America: The Cuban Criminal Pipeline." *Sun Sentinel*. N.d. Web. 27 Sept. 2015. http://interactive. sun-sentinel.com/plundering-america/index.html

O'Matz, Megan. "In Cuba, Fugitive Declines Invitation to Return to U.S." *Sun Sentinel*. 22 Feb. 2015. Web. 27 Sept. 2015. http://www.sun-sentinel.com/ news/nationworld/fl-marshals-service-wanted-cuba-20150222-story.html#page=1 http://www.sun-sentinel. com/news/nationworld/fl-marshals-service-wanted-cuba-20150222-story.html#page=1

Gray, Rosie. "Relative Says Families Of Slain 'Brothers to the Rescue' Weren't Warned of Cuban Spy Release." *Buzzfeed*. 23 Dec. 2014. Web. 27 Sept. 2015. http:// www.buzzfeed.com/rosiegray/relative-says-families-of-slain-brothers-to-the-rescue-weren#.of8O789G5

43938164R00118

Made in the USA
San Bernardino, CA
04 January 2017